UNDER THE GOVERNOR'S SEAL

Book One — The Shape of Power

Mattia Biscontini

Copyright © 2025 Mattia Biscontini

All rights reserved

The characters and events portrayed in this book are fictitious. Any similarity to real persons, living or dead, is coincidental and not intended by the author.

No part of this book may be reproduced, or stored in a retrieval system, or transmitted in any form or by any means, electronic, mechanical, photocopying, recording, or otherwise, without express written permission of the author.

For any enquiries you can contact the author via email at mattiabiscontini@gmail.com

CONTENTS

Title Page
Copyright
Introduction
Preface
Chapter I   1
Chapter II   16
Chapter III   31
Chapter IV   45
Chapter V   58
Chapter VI   71
Chapter VII   85
Chapter VIII   101
Chapter IX   119
Chapter X   133
Chapter XI   148
Chapter XII   164
Chapter XIII   180
Chapter XIV   198
About The Author   223

INTRODUCTION

This is a work of fiction set in and around **1705**. The ports, ships, and politics are drawn from period practice, but I have made deliberate choices for clarity: plain modern English with period **texture** (not a costume of thee/thou), authentic **seamanship** without drowning readers in jargon, and an emphasis on how **papers**, permits, proclamations, letters, could move more weight than gunpowder.

Names and places (Port Royal, Tortuga, Nassau) are used broadly as they were. **Signals, countersigns, and procedures** are plausible rather than archival. **Ranks** and **prize law** are simplified in service of pace, and where the record is silent, such as the exact routines on a given quay, imagination stands in.

I keep British spellings and style ships in italics. If a detail jars you, assume either (a) it's a deliberate modernization for readability, or (b) a period quirk I fell in love with. The moral line here is *no deliberate blood, paper before powder*, is fiction. The way men used **paper to make violence tidy** was not.

Any errors are mine. The sea will forgive them faster than readers will.

PREFACE

From the papers of the Admiralty, Miscellany 1712/37, "Concerning Certain Irregular Proceedings in Jamaica & the Leeward Stations." Transcribed by E. Hawes, Assistant Keeper of Papers.

It is a useful thing, in offices, to remember that **paper is braver than men**. It does not blush, and it does not hang. It bears what it is told to bear, provided the seal is heavy and the ink is dry.

The packet that led to this file arrived from Port Royal in the autumn of 1705, sealed under the Governor's hand and countersigned by a gentleman whose zeal outpaced his pay. It contained, neatly, what most packets pretend to contain: schedules, weather notes, advice upon convoys, a draft of a proclamation, and an opinion disguised as fact.

There was also, bound within, a request that **one Captain William Tyler** be posted in the islands as **deserter and traitor** to the King's peace, and that **Lieutenant Paul Davies** be **confirmed in command of His Majesty's frigate** *Enforcer* until further pleasure be known. The Board, persuaded by furniture as much as argument, consented.

The reader will observe, moving forward, that matters at sea are not governed solely by guns, nor by the courage of men who stand where shot is likely to find them. They are governed by **forms**, by **books that do not leave their tables**, by **permits that make theft lawful** and **names that make murder tidy**. The sea is a great unwritten thing; we write upon it with **orders**.

The papers hereafter—letters, copies, sworn statements, receipts, one sailor's Bible with notes in the margins, and a docket of seized manifests—concern a narrow span of months in which a small number of men discovered that the **shape of power** can be altered by how one **describes** an event, and who is permitted to **describe it first**.

A few advisories for the honest reader:

1. **On Seals & Signatures.** If two documents disagree, believe the one with the better **seal**, unless you know the clerk who warmed the wax. If you know the clerk, believe his private word and distrust both documents.

2. **On Proclamations.** A proclamation posted at a harbour gate is a piece of theatre. The law exists before it and after it; the performance is for the benefit of those who must be seen to agree.

3. **On Pirates & Other Officials.** There are men who take ships and call it piracy. There are men who **lend** the taking a different name and call it office. Their accounts reconcile; do not be surprised.

4. **On Captains Tyler & Davies.** The Board, in its wisdom, prefers captains who obey the book. The sea, in its mood, prefers captains who **obey the weather**. Where these preferences meet, there is sometimes honour, sometimes disaster, and commonly paperwork. What follows shows a little of each.

5. **On a Certain Lost Ship Of The Line.** You will find mention of *Valiant*. If a ship may be both present and absent at once, it is because **paper** can keep a hull alive years after the worms have made another plan. Attend to the dates.

It is not my office to decide who acted well. I am a **keeper**, which is a polite word for a **sweeper**. I sweep up after other men's certainties. I number them as I am told and tie them with ribbon and note in a calm hand that all is in order. It is in order because **we have agreed that it shall be**. Yet I will confess a private inconvenience, being close to these papers: a man comes to know the **hands** before he knows the **faces**.

I know the nervous turn of a clerk who signs **Hartwell**, the measured temper of a lieutenant who writes **S. Greaves** as if he were tucking the page in for sleep, the blunt crossings-out of a quartermaster who refuses to flatter his own spelling.

I know the steady, small lines of a woman who writes like an accountant and thinks like a captain. Their ink speaks. It speaks often against the printed notices nailed to a post. If there is a lesson to be had for those who have never been hungry in a gale or patient in a clerk's lobby, it is this: **Power is not the musket**.

It is the **line** that sets down where the musket may be fired and who shall be thanked afterward. Men can be brave, and still lose to a **paragraph**.

The Board has since reordered the relevant minutes. A later hand has improved certain phrases. A certain hanging is entered as "commended for example." A certain shot discharged under a certain flag is described with **cautionary charity**. There are reasons for all these adjustments. There are always reasons.

The file remains open because ships have a way of continuing even when they stop. The reader will proceed to a series of accounts—some signed, some sworn, some only **believed** until a better lie appears.

Take from them what you like. But remember, as you turn each page, that **the sea keeps few records**; men keep them **for** her, and men are partial creatures. As to **Captain Tyler**, you will make your own judgement. You will weigh a **no-blood rule** against a season in which men were asked to bleed on paper for the comfort of other men's reputations.

You will set a **governor's seal** against the **weather**. And perhaps you will consider, once, how the **shape of power** looks when the seal is pressed **lightly**, and how it looks when a man's thumb stays on the wax a heartbeat too long.

— **E. Hawes,**
Assistant Keeper of Papers, Admiralty
Michaelmas Term, 1712

CHAPTER I

The Last Patrol

August 1705 – East of Port Royal

The day broke brilliant and unyielding, the Caribbean sky a flawless blue stretched across a glassy sea. Winds held steady from the east, filling the sails of His Majesty's frigate *Enforcer* as she shadowed two lumbering merchantmen. Their holds bulged with sugar, rum, spices, and enough wealth to tempt every shark and rogue from Nassau to Tortuga. To a hungry eye, they were as helpless as cattle crossing open pasture: fat, slow, and worth killing for.

Captain William Tyler stood at the *Enforcer*'s helm. His coat of deep navy and gold trim shifted in the breeze, the cut immaculate despite weeks at sea. Beneath his blue tricorn, his powdered wig curled neatly to the collar, though strands had begun to escape in the humid wind. One hand rested lightly on the ship's rail, the other close to the ivory-and-gold hilt of his sword, its balance so familiar he scarcely noticed its weight.

At his left hip, a brown-and-silver pistol gleamed in the morning light, etched with fine golden lines. A personal piece, cared for as carefully as the frigate beneath his feet.

Five years he had commanded the *Enforcer*; ten he had served the Crown. He was not known for cruelty, but for a resolve that brooked no disobedience.

His presence alone kept the deck taut with discipline; his marines, though relaxed in posture, worked with the quiet efficiency of men who knew they were being watched.

Beside him stood Dylan O'Connell, the ship's Quartermaster. Ginger-bearded, barrel-chested, and sharp-eyed.

He carried his authority differently from Tyler; where the captain's was silent, O'Connell's was unmistakable.

He was the voice that cracked across the deck when orders were given, the man who kept the *Enforcer*'s heart beating while Tyler charted its course.

Above, at the masthead, Lieutenant Paul Davies clung to the swaying height with the ease of long practice. His gaze swept the endless horizon, vigilant as ever. Storms, sails, reefs, the distant line of a shore; he had spotted them all before they spotted him. Tyler trusted him implicitly.

The ship herself bore her years openly. Black hull freshly tarred, but here and there patches of newer timber stood out, pale among the dark, repairs from shot and storm alike. Each plank carried memory.

Tyler's eyes lingered on one near the waterline, a broad scar from a fight two years past. For the first time in months, he wondered—not for long, but enough—how many more scars ship or captain might take before the sea claimed them.

Davies' voice cut through the breeze, sharp and unwelcome: "Captain... I see something."

Tyler's head snapped up. He seized his spyglass. "Where away?"

"South-southeast!" Davies called. "Three sails. Moving fast!"

The words tightened every man within earshot.

Conversation died. Even the sea seemed to hush.

Tyler lowered the glass and turned to O'Connell. "Can we make more speed? I'd rather run than crawl if this turns sour."

O'Connell glanced aloft at the canvas, then out to sea, calculations running behind his eyes.

"We're wringing all she's got, Captain. Best wind we'll get. Another point off and we lose what edge we've got."

"Then we stand ready. Signal the convoy—close order, line astern."

Flags climbed swiftly up the halyards. Orders carried down the deck. The *Enforcer* shifted from quiet readiness to purposeful motion: gunports swung open, cannon crews took their places, powder boys scurried from locker to battery.

The merchantmen ahead began to close their distance, lining themselves as ordered. A simple, brutal formation: frigate to the rear, guns outward. The merchants boxed ahead where they might be shielded by broadsides.

Davies' voice rang down again, louder this time: "Black flags, Captain. Two brigs and a sloop."

The air itself seemed to thicken.

Tyler snapped his glass open, tracking the dark smudges drawing nearer, black flags whipping above them. Pirates.

"Mr. O'Connell, load chain shot. I want their sails in the water before they touch us."

"Aye, Captain!" O'Connell turned to the gun crews, his voice a booming command: "Cobbs! Chain shot across all batteries: two volleys ready!"

The gunners responded as one, hauling their weapons into readiness, feeding powder and shot into iron maws.

Tyler exhaled once, controlled, steadily. He had seen pirates before. He knew their hunger. Best to break them fast and hard, show no weakness.

He closed his glass with a snap. "All stations ready. They'll be on us soon enough."

The enemy sails swelled larger with every heartbeat, dark triangles knifing through the blue. Spray leapt from their bows as they bore down at speed. The first of them, a brig to windward, adjusted course hunting the advantage.

"Range?" Tyler called.

"Eight hundred yards, sir!" Davies' reply drifted down from the mast.

Tyler planted a boot on the deck and raised his voice for all to hear. "Stand firm. Let them come to us."

A ripple of tension moved across the crew. Powder monkeys crouched beside their charges, fuses at the ready. Marines took position along the rail, muskets primed. Overhead, the rigging creaked like a ship holding its breath.

"Six hundred!" Davies shouted.

Tyler's hand dropped in a swift, decisive cut. "Fire!"

The *Enforcer* thundered. Sixteen cannons spoke at once, smoke billowing out in a white wall, the air choking with the stench of powder. The sea between the ships erupted in fountains where the chain shot fell.

Through the drifting haze, Tyler's eyes sought damage. The pirates scattered, breaking formation to weave through the onslaught. The lead brig's sails bore slashes, but she kept her speed.

"Minimal damage!" Davies called.

"Reload. Hold for angle," Tyler ordered evenly.

The gun crews worked with relentless precision. Ramrods

thudded; powder hissed into pans. Tyler waited, calculating vectors, wind, and distance. Patience won battles. Panic lost them.

The brig to leeward overcommitted, cutting too close.

"Now," Tyler said.

The second broadside tore through the morning. This time the result was unmistakable: a mainmast shattered like a struck match. The brig staggered, momentum dying as her canvas collapsed. A cheer began on deck—but O'Connell's bark cut it dead.

"Reload! Round shot! On my mark!"

The two remaining foes charged, one straight on, the other angling to rake across the convoy. Enemy fire answered. Shot slammed into the *Enforcer*'s starboard side, jolting her. Wood splintered; a man cried out and was dragged below by the surgeon's mates.

"Report!" Tyler snapped.

"Two guns down, three men hurt!" came the reply.

Tyler's voice was iron. "Focus fire on the brig. Break her teeth before she breaks ours."

"Aye!" O'Connell roared. "All batteries, target the brig!"

The next broadside landed true. Iron punched through timber. One shot found a powder keg: the brig bloomed in fire and smoke, her deck vanishing in a shower of debris.

The sea around her boiled with flame, but there was no time to celebrate.

The sloop had slipped wide of the fight and was now alongside the lead merchantman. Grapples flew. Pirates swarmed her deck like ants.

"Full speed!" Tyler barked. "Prepare to board!"

The *Enforcer* heeled slightly as O'Connell drove her ahead.

Boarding axes, cutlasses, and muskets were passed hand to hand. Men tightened straps, checked powder, kissed tokens hung around necks.

"Mr. Davies!" Tyler called.

"Sir?"

"With me."

The frigate slammed alongside the sloop. Boarding planks clattered down.

"Forward!" Tyler's order rang like steel.

Blue-coated marines surged across the gap, muskets firing into the melee ahead. Tyler followed with sword drawn, O'Connell at his side, and Davies just behind. The merchant's deck was chaos—pistols cracking, steel on steel, screams mixing with shouted orders.

Tyler cut down a pirate who lunged at him, his blade biting deep. "Push them back! Secure the hatch!" he shouted over the din. Davies' voice joined his, hoarse but fierce: "Press on, men!"

Step by brutal step, the Navy drove the boarders to the rail. Blood slicked the planks. Smoke burned throats. A final rush broke their line entirely. Most fell where they stood. The rest tried to flee and were cut down.

Only one pirate remained, cornered, holding the merchant captain in front of him like a shield, knife pressed to the man's throat. His grin was a twisted mask of defiance.

Tyler leveled his pistol. "Drop it," he said, voice low and lethal. "You're finished. Die here or hang in Port Royal for all to see."

The pirate laughed—a quiet, unsettling sound. "Captain William Tyler," he said, savoring the name. "Soul of the *Enforcer*.

Blade of the Crown. Oh, we know you."

Tyler's eyes narrowed. "Do you."

"Aye." The man's head turned toward the open sea. "And so does he."

Tyler followed the motion and saw it.

A fourth ship. Larger. Watching from beyond the haze, sails furled but ready. At her bow stood a man of medium build, one boot on the railing, arms folded on his raised knee. Dark curls stirred in the wind around a face marked by a long scar running from left eye to chin. A pipe hung from his lips, smoke spiraling lazily upward. Above him flew a flag black as night: skull, sword, and pistol crossed beneath.

Jack 'The Scarred'.

The pirate captain's gaze met Tyler's across the water. He inhaled slowly, then exhaled a curl of smoke. "William Tyler!" he called, voice carrying clear and calm. "We finally meet."

Tyler's pistol never wavered, but his tone dropped to something quieter, sharper. "To what do I owe this pleasure, Jack?"

"Pleasure?" he said. "That's generous. Let's call it necessity. You wouldn't come if I invited, would you?"

He nodded once toward his man, who shoved the merchant captain away and bolted for the sloop's rail. Then Jack raised his voice again, clear and commanding: "Now, Captain… five of yours, five of mine. Neutral ground. Your quarters."

Tyler's finger twitched on the trigger. "Or," he said evenly, "I put a bullet through your head right here."

Jack chuckled, low and amused, like a man hearing a familiar joke. "And then both ships open fire," he said, pipe never leaving his lips. "Your convoy sinks. Those fat merchants you've bled to protect? Gone. And you—Commodore-in-waiting, they tell me—watch your career drown with them. Shall we test who blinks first?"

The silence that followed was suffocating. Every man on the *Enforcer* felt it, from the masthead to the gundeck. Tyler's eyes stayed locked on Jack's. He weighed the risk, the promise, the cost.

At length, he holstered his pistol. "Mr. Davies," he said. "Choose four men. The rest, back to stations."

Inside Tyler's quarters, the air hung heavily with salt, smoke, and the tang of iron from his sword rack. The cabin had been cleared; outside, ten armed men formed two rigid lines; five Navy, five pirates. Within, only Tyler and Jack remained, though the latter made himself quite at home.

Jack swung into the chair behind Tyler's desk, propped his boots up, and reached for the decanter without asking. He poured generously, tossed back a swallow, and sighed with theatrical satisfaction. "Sit, Captain," he said. "Have a drink. You've earned it."

Tyler remained standing, hands clasped behind his back. "I'll stand. Talk."

Jack smirked and lit his pipe anew. Smoke drifted between them like a third presence. "Word is," he began casually, "your governor's gone rotten. Not in the usual, predictable way: skimming, bribes, the occasional 'missing' shipment. No. He's in bed with my kind. Not privateers. Pirates. The kind who bleed towns dry and leave them to rot."

Tyler's expression didn't flicker. "And why tell me this? You profit from chaos."

Jack leaned forward, elbows on knees. The grin was gone

now, replaced by a predator's calm. "Not this chaos. Their game kills mine. I like order, Captain, the kind I can manipulate. This?" He jabbed the air with his pipe. "This makes the whole board worthless."

"Proof," Tyler said, voice flat.

Jack reached into his coat and tossed a bundle of papers onto the desk. They landed with a soft thud. "Read."

Tyler picked them up, scanning quickly. His eyes caught on names, dates, and sums—and then the seal. A deep-red blob of wax impressed with the unmistakable Royal arms. His stomach tightened.

"These could be forged," he said, but the words felt hollow even as he spoke them.

Jack tapped the seal with his pipe stem. "Royal. Straight from Port Royal's own offices. Look at it, Tyler. Look and tell me you believe otherwise."

"If you burn those papers, only my word stands," Jack said mildly. "If you keep them, so does your doubt."

Tyler's jaw clenched. He looked again, and the weight of the truth pressed harder. If this was real—and God help him, it looked real—it meant rot at the very core of the administration he had served faithfully for ten years.

"Why me?" he asked finally, voice low.

Jack leaned back, smoke curling lazily from his lips. "Because you've seen cracks in the walls and kept pretending they weren't there. Because you're about to wear a Commodore's coat, and I wanted to speak to you before you sell your soul to the very devils you fight. My birds tell me you're a loyal man. Good. Stay that way. You'll be useful."

A chill ran through Tyler's chest, cold as the sea in winter.

If Jack knew this much, someone close, someone trusted, was feeding him.

"What do you expect me to do with this?"

"Right now?" Jack spread his hands. "Nothing. Later, when you've got the power to make it hurt, you'll owe me. Until then, enjoy your shore leave. Hug your wife. Kiss your children. As if nothing changed."

Tyler stared at him, searching for deceit, finding none. Only a man who held the cards and knew it.

At last, he turned on his heel. "We're done here."

Jack raised his glass in a lazy salute as Tyler opened the door. "Until next time, Commodore."

Outside, Davies caught a glimpse of his captain's face as he emerged: a face carved from stone, but with something underneath. Worry. Disbelief. Questions without answers. He said nothing, merely saluted as Tyler passed.

The pirates withdrew, and the convoy pushed on. The sun slid toward the horizon, gilding the calm sea in gold. To anyone else, it looked as though nothing had happened.

Below, however, something had changed. Lieutenant Davies lingered at the rail, watching his captain vanish into the cabin. He had seen Tyler's face after the parley; a mask of stone with a crack beneath. Unease twisted in his gut.

After a moment, he went below to the lower gunroom. The makeshift mess buzzed with low voices around an upturned barrel that served as a table. O'Connell sat grinning over his cards; opposite him, Gideon Cobbs, grey at the temples, thick hands scarred by years at the guns; beside them, Arthur Jenkins, quiet as a shadow, short fair hair in need of a trim, right index finger missing from a misfire in training.

Davies stepped into the lamplight. "Evening, gentlemen."

"Lieutenant," Cobbs muttered, not looking up.

"Come to lose your rations again?" O'Connell said, flashing a grin.

"Not tonight." Davies leaned to the bulkhead, arms folded. "Needed company after a long day in that little round bucket."

O'Connell chuckled.

"At least I don't piss myself climbing into it, unlike someone else." Davies jerked a thumb toward Jenkins.

The boy flushed scarlet. "That was once," he muttered.

"Leave him be," O'Connell said, laughing. "He's still got both legs. For now."

Laughter rolled around the barrel, then ebbed. Davies lowered his voice. "You all saw the captain after that meeting with The Scarred."

O'Connell's grin faded. "Aye. Had to ask him the same question twice. He was somewhere else entirely. I figured the promotion was gnawing at him."

"Maybe," Davies said. "But when he came out, I saw papers on his desk. Official seals. Not the sort pirates carry."

Cobbs set his cards down. "Then best we don't sniff around. Whatever it is, he'll tell us when he's ready."

Silence settled. The lantern flickered; shadows swayed along the planks.

"Maybe," Jenkins said softly, eyes on his hand. "But seals don't just show up on a captain's desk for nothing."

O'Connell shot him a look. "Don't start, lad."

"I'm just saying…" Jenkins murmured, voice trailing off.

The cards resumed, but the air had changed. Questions hung unspoken as the sea carried them toward home.

By sunset, the sea had smoothed to molten gold. The *Enforcer* sailed on in disciplined silence, escorting her charges toward safety. The patched frigate bore new scars—splintered timber, two ruined guns—but she held her dignity, as did her captain, though within him something had come loose...

Tyler stood at the quarterdeck rail; gaze fixed on the horizon ahead. The battle was over, the convoy secure, yet his thoughts circled like gulls around the papers in his cabin. That seal. That truth he'd tried to deny for years and now could no longer.

Footsteps approached softly behind him. "Strange, isn't it?" O'Connell's voice was quieter than usual. "Last time aboard the *Enforcer*. You should be savoring it, Captain."

Tyler's lips twitched into what passed for a smile. "Perhaps I will... when we're ashore."

O'Connell studied him a moment, then returned to his duties.

Dawn broke pale and clear. Land rose ahead, dark against the soft light: Port Royal. The frigate eased toward the harbour with the grace of long practice, sails furled, ropes coiled, decks scrubbed even after battle. Tyler gave his final commands with a steady voice, though he had not slept a moment.

On a low hill overlooking the bay stood his home: a modest, white-walled house framed by palms, its garden sloping toward the sea. Sarah had stood there every morning in his absence, watching for his return. She stood there now, parasol closed at her side, eyes searching. When she spotted the silhouette of a frigate against the dawn, her heart quickened.

She turned inside, voice ringing: "Tom! Lizzie! Wake up, your father's home!"

Within minutes, she was dressed in a crimson day gown, wide-brimmed hat shading her face, gloves immaculate. She gathered the children and set off down the path to the docks.

On the pier, the *Enforcer* kissed the dock with practiced precision. Sailors leapt ashore, securing lines. The crew spilled into motion—offloading cargo, logging damage, preparing for repair.

Harbourmaster Tobias Keane approached, ledger under his arm, grinning through weathered wrinkles. "Captain Tyler! Welcome back!"

"Mr. Keane," Tyler replied, descending the gangway. "Here for the damage report?"

"Aye. And to see you in one piece. Quiet voyage?"

"Calm enough," Tyler said, eyes flicking toward the patched hull. "Until three pirate vessels tried their luck. One boarded a merchantman; we saw them off. Quartermaster O'Connell will provide the details."

"Much obliged," Keane said, and moved toward the quarterdeck.

Tyler's gaze swept the pier and found her. Sarah.

Even at a distance, he knew her shape as surely as the *Enforcer*'s silhouette. She walked with poise, Tom tugging eagerly at her hand, little Lizzie clinging to her brother. Her blonde curls glinted beneath her hat, her green eyes bright as polished emerald. When they met his across the bustle of the dock, time seemed to slow.

"Father!" Tom's voice rang out, high and joyous. He tore free and sprinted down the pier.

"Come here, son," Tyler called, crouching, arms open. The boy collided with him in a fierce embrace.

"Have you kept your promise? Been the man of the house?"

"I did, Father! Ask Mother!"

Sarah reached them then. She and Tyler locked eyes for a heartbeat that said more than words. Then she stepped into him, and he wrapped her in his arms.

"We missed you," she whispered.

He kissed her once, then scooped Lizzie up. She giggled and clung to his neck.

Sarah had kept his presence alive by reading his letters aloud, telling stories of the sea, never letting their father become a stranger.

O'Connell's voice boomed from above. "Captain, we're all done here, sir."

He caught sight of the family and winced. "Ah... my apologies, Mrs. Tyler. I didn't mean to intrude."

Sarah smiled up at him. "Don't worry, Mr. O'Connell; I'll have my husband all to myself soon enough."

"Much obliged, ma'am," O'Connell said with a grin. "Captain, permission for the lads and me to pay our respects to the Old Lord?"

Tyler's mouth curved faintly. "Permission granted. Try to behave."

"I'll do my best, sir. No promises past the second bottle," O'Connell said with a lopsided salute.

"Just don't make the guards drag you out. I've no wish to spend the night in a cell covering for you," Tyler replied dryly.

The crew erupted in cheers as liberty was granted, streaming off toward Port Royal's infamous taverns.

Tyler slipped an arm around Sarah's waist. Together with their children, they began the walk home.

As they walked away from the docks, Tyler cast one last glance over his shoulder. The *Enforcer* lay still at berth, her patched hull glinting in the late sun. Beyond her masts, on a far warehouse roof, a lone figure stood.

A boy, no older than twelve, with a scarlet kerchief tied around his head.

The moment Tyler's eyes found him, the boy touched two fingers to his brow, turned, and slipped behind the chimney.

Tyler said nothing to Sarah. But inside, he knew: Jack's reach had already come ashore.

Behind them, the *Enforcer* lay moored, silent and scarred, her secrets locked below decks… for now.

To the casual eye, nothing had happened. But inside Tyler, the world had shifted.

CHAPTER II

The Viper's Nest

Sarah pushed open the front door, and the familiar scent of lavender rolled over Tyler like a tide. It was exactly as he remembered. She had left in such haste that the children's nightclothes still littered the floor, but he didn't care. He was home.

Sarah ushered the children upstairs to change, while Tyler prepared for the bath. Shedding his salt-stained coat felt like dropping an anchor. Moments later he sank into the steaming water, civilian clothes folded neatly on a chair.

The warmth eased muscles long hardened by wind and duty. For a rare moment, his mind was silent.

In the kitchen, Sarah chopped vegetables for chicken and potato soup, the laughter of Tom and Lizzie carrying in through the open window as they played in the yard.

Tyler padded in quietly, still damp, a towel his only cover. "I missed you," he murmured, arms circling her waist.

She set the knife aside and turned, looping her arms around his neck.

"I missed you too… more than you can know."

Their lips met in a lingering kiss.

"I dreamed of this day," she whispered. "You home from your last mission. I want you here every morning when I make your favorite breakfast, every afternoon for tea by the fire… and every night, sharing the bed with the man I fell in love with."

Tyler's smile was faint, almost wistful. "We'll see our children grow. And probably argue about their education."

Sarah brushed a finger across his jaw. "Go get dressed, Captain. Lunch won't make itself."

Upstairs, Tyler changed into fresh clothes and unlocked a small brass-handled door at the end of the hall; his private room, forbidden to others.

Inside, a narrow window poured muted light over a polished wooden desk, a wedding gift from his father. Beside it sat a stout old chest.

In the far corner, a mannequin wore his grandfather's naval coat, preserved like a relic. Faded now to pale blue, its gold trim still caught the light. It was more than fabric; it was lineage. His family had served the Crown for generations, from his great-grandfather, an admiral, down to his own father.

Tyler rested his own pistol and sword on a second mannequin bearing his "Official Business" uniform—dark coat, gold trim—reserved for church Sundays or meetings with men of influence.

"Lunch is ready!" Sarah's call reached him. He locked the door behind him and descended to the dining room.

For the first time in months, they sat as a family around the same table. It felt sacred. They joined hands; heads bowed.

"Dear Lord," Sarah prayed, her voice steady, "thank You for this food, for our health, and for the strength to meet life's trials. Amen."

The soup was humble: chicken, potatoes, garden vegetables, but to Tyler it was a feast. Each spoonful tasted like home, like earth. For a moment, he believed this peace might hold.

Then came three precise knocks at the door—sharp, deliberate.

The air shifted.

"I'll see who it is. Eat," Sarah said, rising.

She opened the door to find a pale man in morning light, round spectacles perched on a pointed nose, tall black hat shadowing his face.

His attire was as severe as his expression: black coat, pale grey gloves with a faint silvery sheen. Behind him stood a carriage bearing the governor's insignia.

"Is Mr. Tyler at home, my dear?" His voice was low, smooth, and cold, like silk over a knife. "I have matters of importance to discuss."

"And you are…?" Sarah asked, polite but wary.

"Oh, where are my manners?" The man's smile never reached his eyes. "Edward Norton, counsellor to the governor."

The name needed no introduction. Norton was whispered across the Caribbean, loathed in taverns and officer's messes alike. Jack 'The Scarred' had called him a weasel. That had been kind.

Norton was worse: venom in human form, every word a barbed hook wrapped in silk.

"Pleased to meet you, Mr. Norton. I'm Sarah," she said evenly.

"Would you like to come in? We were just having lunch."

"Thank you, my dear. I shall gladly stop for a few minutes, eat something, and speak with your husband."

She led him to the dining room and opened the double doors.

"William," she said, "Mr. Norton is here for you."

The name and the sight of him drained the colour from

Tyler's face. His stomach lurched. *Why is he here? Why not a letter? Does he know about Jack?*

Norton was already seated by the time Tyler reached the table, posture immaculate, eyes scanning the room like a ledger.

He did not remove his hat.

"Captain Tyler," Norton said smoothly.

"What a pleasure to have you back. First, allow me to compliment your modest home—and your charming wife."

His gaze drifted across the room, measuring. "It feels... fitting for someone like you."

Every syllable weighed to belittle.

"Mr. Norton," Tyler replied evenly. "To what do I owe the visit?"

"This matter could not be handled by letter," Norton said.

"It required a personal touch. But first—" his gaze flicked to the table "—do you have anything to drink? My throat is dry from the day's work."

Tyler fetched one of his finest rums. Men like Norton never asked for water. He poured it and set it before him.

"This is my best."

"That will do." Norton took it without saying thanks.

Sarah returned with a steaming bowl of soup and set it down. He tasted it, paused just long enough to sting.

"Remarkable," he said.

"I have always wondered how some manage such flavor from such... simple ingredients."

Sarah's smile tightened. "Children, with me," she said evenly, and led Tom and Lizzie out, though her eyes burned as she glanced back.

Tyler put down his spoon. His appetite was gone.

Norton set the glass down with care, folding his hands neatly before him. "Let's not waste time, Captain. Allow me to speak plainly."

"You have my attention," Tyler replied.

"I regret to burden you so soon after your return," Norton said, voice smooth as oiled steel, "but not everyone was as fortunate as you. The HMS *Valiant*, along with her captain and crew, has vanished in the waters we call The Passage."

The words hit like cannon fire. Tyler's face hardened.

"Who commanded her?"

"Adrian Stevens," Norton said, watching Tyler closely. "A fine officer. Left behind a wife and child. Did you know him?"

"I cannot say I did," Tyler answered evenly. "But I would honor his family, as the Crown surely will."

"I am afraid the Crown will not—at least not publicly," Norton replied, each word meant.

Tyler's control cracked.

"Excuse me? What will you tell his wife and child? That he still lives? That letters will come from beyond the grave? This is —"

"Mr. Tyler," Norton cut in sharply, his voice like a blade through canvas.

"Compose yourself. There is more at stake than a single family's grief. We have no confirmation of the *Valiant*'s fate. No wreckage. No bodies. Until we do, she is not lost... merely unaccounted for."

"Also," Norton continued, unbothered, "if we were to make this public, every pirate in those waters would know there is no major resistance. The Passage would become chaos overnight. Is that what you want?"

"I understand," Tyler said aloud. Inside, his thoughts roiled. *Every time I turn my head, the Crown finds a new way to blind me. How much rot must I serve before I drown in it?*

"And that," Norton said, slicing through his thoughts, "brings me to why I am here. The Crown promised you a desk, yes... but circumstances have changed. We need someone to patrol The Passage and uncover what happened to the *Valiant*."

Tyler felt the future he had imagined only hours earlier: quiet mornings, evenings by the fire, watching his children grow, splinter like a mast under chain shot.

Norton reached into his coat, producing a letter sealed in deep red wax.

"The Governor expects you tomorrow evening. This is your summons. Do not be late."

Tyler took it without looking, his mind a storm of images and unanswered questions.

"Of course," he said finally, the word tasting like ash.

Norton rose, placing his napkin precisely on the table.

"Thank you for the meal, Mrs. Tyler," he called smoothly as Sarah re-entered. "And Captain... welcome home."

The front door closed softly behind him, but its echo lingered.

Tyler remained seated, staring at nothing.

He wanted desperately to believe this was a nightmare, that he would wake up to find Sarah in the kitchen, soup still warm, children laughing outside. But the weight in his chest told him otherwise.

Tyler reached for the bundle of papers Jack had given him at sea, hidden in his coat pocket. For a moment, he considered throwing them into the fire, ending it all: no secrets, no leverage, no excuses left to bind him.

His hand hovered over the hearth. But he didn't. He shoved them back into his coat, jaw tight. *I can't... not yet.*

The sea was calling him back. Not as an invitation. As a summons.

The Passage—Crown shorthand for the *Windward Passage*—the narrow strait between *Cuba* and *Hispaniola* that sailors call the Red Zone. No merchant dared cross it. Ships entered and never returned. It was a hunting ground where pirates struck like wolves and Navy blood mingled with theirs in stalemate after stalemate.

And the *Valiant*? Not some light frigate, but a ship of the line. Sixty guns. Thirty a side. Broadside enough to tear a brigantine in half... gone. Vanished without wreckage, without survivors.

How, Tyler thought, could a ship like that simply disappear?

Sarah entered quietly.

She stopped at the sight of him: rigid, unmoving, eyes like stone.

The strongest man she knew, staring into nothing.

"What did he say?" she asked, voice tight.

"There is no desk for me," Tyler said softly. He extended the sealed letter. Sarah broke the wax and read aloud:

For the attention of Captain William Tyler,

I, Sir Thomas Sevington, request your presence tomorrow at five o'clock. Mr. Norton will have briefed you on the situation.
The matter is of utmost urgency and secrecy. A government carriage will be sent for you.

Signed,

Sir Thomas Sevington, Governor of Port Royal

She lowered the letter slowly; eyes fixed on him. "Why? What happened?"

"I cannot tell you yet, my dear," Tyler replied quietly.

"I will not accept this, William. You cannot accept this!" Her voice broke, tears brimming.

"They promised… you promised… we would be a normal family. I cannot live in fear of the day a letter comes saying you're dead!"

Tyler rose and gathered her in his arms, holding her against him. "I know, love," he murmured. "I know."

Later, as dusk settled, Tyler stood by the window, Sarah asleep upstairs, the letter from Sevington on the table beside him. Hoofbeats echoed faintly in the street below.

A carriage passed slowly, unmarked. Its driver cloaked, face hidden in the dim light. Tyler's hand twitched toward the pistol on the mantel, but the carriage rolled on, vanishing into the dark.

He exhaled slowly. *Paranoia*, he told himself. *Or the first sign I'm already trapped.* He glanced to the rooftops, no scarlet kerchief.

The Governor's Residence – Later that day…

The echo of hurried footsteps carried through the black-and-grey marble corridors of the Governor's residence. Sunlight streamed through towering windows, glinting off polished stone until the floor shone like a still pond.

Edward Norton walked swiftly, face-composed, purpose set. He had returned from his errands and was ready to report.

The main hall doors groaned open. Inside, the Governor's chamber sprawled in gaudy opulence. A long table stretched nearly the entire length of the room, its carved golden legs gleaming.

Marble statues lined the walls, sharing space with oil paintings: pastoral scenes, the Governor's own likeness, and, most prominently, His Majesty's portrait.

A vast fireplace dominated one wall; its mantel crowded with gilded ornaments. Above, an ambitious mosaic covered the ceiling, crowned by a massive golden chandelier heavy with crystal.

At the far end sat Governor Sir Thomas Sevington. Heir to one of Port Royal's wealthiest families, his power had been bought with slave-trade fortunes and cemented by ruthless loyalty to the Crown. He leaned back in a gilded chair, a roasted chicken leg in his left hand while his right flicked through a ledger. Grease stained the pages; crumbs dotted the wood.

"Governor, I have returned," Norton announced, his voice carrying across the vast chamber.

Sevington glanced up briefly, then gestured to the liveried servant beside him to leave. The doors shut softly, sealing them in.

"Edward," Sevington said, his tone a mixture of impatience and boredom. "At last. How did it go?"

"I visited the docks and taverns as ordered," Norton replied. "Agent Ogdenville reported nothing of note. Lieutenant Greaves observed movement near the barber shop—two arrests were made. I also delivered the summons to Tyler. He said little, but he was... unsettled. I am not certain we can rely on him."

That caught Sevington's attention. The chicken paused mid-bite.

"Go on."

"He is shaken, Governor. Distracted. His reputation for obedience may not hold. I suspect he may have doubts about us."

Sevington tapped the ledger with a wine-stained finger, voice quickening with interest.

"Look here, Edward. The harbourmaster's account of the *Enforcer*. Tyler brought the convoy intact. The profits more than cover the losses. Repairs are trivial. We need him. Efficiency like his is rare." His smile widened, flushed with wine and greed.

"We cannot afford to put him behind a desk."

"My thoughts exactly, sir," Norton said.

"How shall we keep him in line? Make him think this is an honor rather than a leash?"

Norton's lips curved faintly. "We present it as a distinction. Promise it's temporary; six months at most. If he resists, I'll step in. We can use Mrs. Gretchen again… she still owes you. She'll prepare a forged document with the King's stamp. I'll dictate the content."

Sevington smirked. "It wouldn't be her first forgery. She's quite skilled now. And yes, she still owes me for placing her son. See to it."

Norton inclined his head. "At once, sir."

He turned sharply and left, footsteps echoing in the marble hall.

The day after – Tyler's house…

Rain began in thin, scattered drops by afternoon, the first edge of a coming storm. Grey light dulled the sea beyond Port

Royal's bay, and the house stood still in its shadow.

In his private room, Tyler readied himself. He opened the chest and removed his parade pistol, polishing the brass hilt streaked with pale veins until it gleamed. He set it carefully on the floor.

Next came the parade sword; a fine weapon, single golden vein running from tip to guard, engraved with: *The brave men do not fear duty*. Its white cord handle remained pristine. That, too, he laid beside the pistol.

From the chest he drew a small square box, placing it on the desk. Inside lay his medals: *To Valor, To Duty, To Discipline*. Silent testaments to years of service.

Finally, his eyes lifted to the mannequin. He reached for the coat and tricorn hat. The coat's deep, electric blue still held its dignity, trimmed in ivory and buttoned in gold. He wore cream breeches, and the black boots gleamed beneath their gilded buckles.

He dressed without hesitation, belted pistol to his right, and sword to his left. Outside, the distant clop of hooves grew louder: the governor's carriage approaching.

Tyler placed his medals briefly to his chest, a private ritual, then donned white gloves and descended the stairs.

"Promise me one thing, William," Sarah said quietly at the door.

He paused, meeting her eyes.

"You will not stand for it."

A beat. Then a single, firm nod.

Without a word, he stepped out into the rain.

The carriage arrived precisely, as governor's business always did.

Tyler opened the door, climbed in, and sat stiffly. Hands resting on his thighs, gaze locked on the rain-streaked window. Not even the jolt of wheels over cobblestone disturbed him.

By the time the carriage rolled to a stop, the governor's residence loomed ahead, pompous and vast, dripping wealth. A guard opened the door.

Tyler gave him a curt nod, mounted the stone steps, and knocked twice on the main office door.

"Come in," came the voice from within.

Inside, Governor Sevington sat behind a massive desk, the smug oil portrait of himself hanging overhead like a silent witness.

Norton lingered by the window, hands clasped behind his back, watching the rain streak down the glass.

"Please, Captain, have a seat," Sevington said, voice too smooth.

"Drink?" Norton offered, already pouring one for himself.

"I avoid drink while on duty, Mr. Norton," Tyler replied.

"A wise choice," Norton said mildly. "One not everyone shares. Sets you apart."

Sevington leaned forward. "First, let me personally congratulate you, Captain. The convoy's success is no small feat. You have the Crown's gratitude."

Tyler gave a single nod.

"I believe Mr. Norton has already explained why you're here," Sevington continued.

"Yes, sir. The *Valiant* is gone, and you want me to patrol The Passage and discover what happened."

"Precisely. You are our best hope. I know we promised you a desk, but circumstances have changed. We need you at sea."

Tyler's voice sharpened. "And what exactly are you asking of me?"

"One final mission," Sevington said. "Six months, perhaps a year at most. Find out what happened. Keep The Passage in check until London sends reinforcements."

Tyler leaned back slightly, eyes narrowing. "Pardon me, sir, but isn't this suicide? A ship of the line like the *Valiant* couldn't survive, and you expect a frigate like *Enforcer* to? We'd be the main prize."

"This is all we can give you," Sevington replied flatly. "Perhaps another frigate will come in three months, but no sooner."

Tyler's voice dropped, low and dangerous.

"With respect, sir, I've served faithfully for fifteen years. I earned my promotion. I earned time with my family. And now you would keep me at sea. I demand to speak with London directly."

Norton moved before Sevington could respond: "The order came from London, Captain," he said smoothly, stepping forward. "You've been entrusted with the colonies' safety. You cannot refuse."

He handed Tyler a letter sealed with red wax, the royal seal.

Tyler broke it, eyes scanning: the wax held the Royal arms, perfect… too perfect. A tiny smear along the rim where no clerk in Whitehall would leave one.

Dear Captain William Tyler,

It is with reluctance that we ask you to serve again, but the colonies need you once more.

We have received, in secrecy, the news of the Valiant's disappearance. This must remain classified.
Find out what happened and report directly. Your promotion is postponed until the mission's completion.

Signed,
Lords Commissioners of the Admiralty

A turn of phrase snagged him: odd, clipped, not quite the Admiralty's usual hand. He shoved the doubt aside.

Tyler's pulse thudded in his ears. This wasn't just Sevington's scheme; London itself had bound him. Refusal meant ruin, acceptance meant sailing straight into death.

"So, Captain," Norton said softly, "shall we proceed with the mission details?"

But the words blurred. Tyler's dam broke.

"I will not accept this!" His fists slammed the desk, rattling inkwell and quills.

Sevington flinched, startled. Norton remained utterly still.

"Excuse me, Captain?!" Sevington barked, face flushing.

"Are you refusing a direct order of the Crown? Do you grasp what that means? The destruction of your career, your name—perhaps even your life!"

Tyler met his glare unblinking. "I have been loyal. I have always said yes. I have given sweat, blood, and years. All I ask is what I've earned."

"Gentlemen," Norton interjected smoothly, like oil on water. "No need for this heat. Captain, take some time. Be with your family. Then give us your answer."

Tyler straightened, jaw set. "I will... but before I go, know this: I am aware of your dealings with pirates, Norton. I have proof." His voice was low, each word a blade.

Norton's face didn't change, but something flickered in his eyes.

"Careful, Captain," he said evenly. "Accusations like that can be… costly."

Tyler saluted sharply, turned on his heel, and left. The door closed behind him with solid finality.

Inside, silence hung for a moment.

"This is outrageous," Sevington spat.

"The letter should have convinced him, and now he dares accuse us?"

"As I said," Norton replied calmly, "we cannot count on him. The forged summons would sway any other man. But Tyler… he's not only resisting; he's dangerous, and I will use his own mistake to destroy him. He met with Jack 'The Scarred' at sea. My informants heard it whispered. His crew saw them together. One of them will talk if pressed."

Sevington's scowl deepened. "Interrogate them?"

"Not overtly," Norton said.

"I'll call it an intelligence review. Ask about pirate activity, infiltration… mix truth with suggestion until one slips. Then we'll have a statement tying Tyler to Jack, backed by 'witnesses' and forged correspondence, ironclad. Once rumors grow, we present the case to the Crown. Tyler will hang as a traitor. Clean and bloodless."

Sevington leaned back, a grin creeping onto his face: "Elegant, Edward. Very elegant."

CHAPTER III

Cornered

The storm crept in from the horizon, slow but relentless. Winds rose, rain thickened, and the sky bruised to iron. The harbour lost its edges, rope and post and hull turning into wet shapes. The smell of tar and wet hemp filled the lane.

Tyler sat by the heart, a glass of whisky loose in his hand, eyes fixed on the flames as if they were holding answers. Heat licked his shins; the rest of him felt made of cold iron.

The governor's words still rang in his skull, heavier each time he replayed them. He hadn't told Sarah—not yet. How do you break, aloud, the life you promised?

Laughter carried from the next room: Sarah playing with the children, keeping spirits bright while rain rattled the panes. Tom's high certainty, Lizzie's bright laughter.

A pot simmered on the hook: onion and salt and something from her Sarah's cousin garden, breath of warmth against the iron smell of outside. A drip from the lintel ticked into a bowl set there for the purpose, regular as a metronome.

At last, Tyler stood, climbed the stairs, and paused at the bedroom door. He laid a palm on the jamb, counted to four, then breathed.

"Sarah," he said quietly. "We need to talk."

"Tom, watch Lizzie while your father and I speak," she told

their son, not turning from the little paper soldiers she had placed in a small line on the dresser. Her hair was still damp from the earlier dash to bring in the washing, curling at the ends.

"You can count on me, Mother," Tom said with the solemn pride of a boy entrusted with a man's duty. Lizzie huffed, decided that being counted on was boring, and went back to making two buttons clack like horses.

They went down to the fire. For a long moment Tyler stared at it, then spoke.

"They've ordered me on another mission. Six months to a year. The Passage."

Sarah's head snapped up. The fire put gold in her eyes. "What did you tell them?"

"I told them no, just as you said." He exhaled.

"But… the order came from London directly."

"Then we write to London," Sarah said. "If we explain the situation the Admiralty will—"

"It's too late." Tyler cut in, gentle but firm.

"A letter would take weeks we don't have." Outside, a gust shoved the rain sideways; the shutter thudded and then held.

"Why?"

"Because if I refuse, I'll be imprisoned… or worse," he said flatly.

"If I go, I may never return while if I stay, I risk everything another way."

Sarah crossed to the window, arms folded, storm light veiling her face. She did not drag the curtain; she watched the smear of lanterns across the lane. Instead of pleading, her voice was steel.

"If my husband must die at sea, I'd rather he dies aa a free man."

The words hit like shot.

"You want me to become... a pirate?"

"Not a pirate," she said, turning. Her eyes were fierce.

"A symbol. A man who stood against rot. Someone they fear. You've been loyal, and they've given you nothing. I won't be the next captain's widow."

She set her hand on the table next to his, not touching, sharing heat.

"It's time, William. No more turning your head. On your honor... promise me."

He stared, stunned by how sure she sounded. He heard the bowl's patient drip and the small shift of Tom on the stairs.

"I promise," he said at last.

"No more doing the Crown's bidding. I'll become a ghost, hunting truth and putting it where they can't silence it. They chose the wrong man to betray."

A spark returned to his eyes. "You and the children should leave tonight. In this weather, no one will follow."

"I'm not leaving," Sarah said, steady.

"I'll support you from land, my cousin can hide us. I'll write, spread the truth."

"The governor has eyes in every post house," he warned. "Use only trusted couriers and never the same twice."

"I'll find them," she replied.

"Are you certain? I'll have no peace knowing you're in danger for me."

"Don't worry about us, William," she said.

"Do what you must... and be free."

She took a small silver locket from her pocket, their initials engraved faint as breath.

"Take this. Remember who you're fighting for, and what waits when you come back."

Tyler closed his hand over it, feeling the warmth of her touch in the metal.

"First, I'll speak with my officers. If they stand with me, the rest will follow." He put the locket under his shirt where the chain would not glint.

Tom crept two steps down and peered through the banister.

"Do we need to pack my shells?" he whispered, then looked proud of how small his whisper was.

"Two," Sarah said without turning. "And the blue marble. No arguing."

Lizzie, who had not been invited to whisper, held up her buttons like medals.

"I have three." She looked at her father, read the set of his shoulders, and tucked them in her apron without being told.

Tyler found the edge of a smile and let it go. He touched the lintel as they passed back toward the stairs, the way sailors touch a mast on leaving harbour.

William Tyler, obedient servant of the Crown, was already fading. In his place, something more dangerous took shape: not just a man, but an idea.

The next day – The Old Lord...

The storm had swallowed Port Royal whole. Rain lashed the streets; tavern lanterns swung on their hooks.

The Old Lord's windows fogged and dripped, but inside warmth and chaos defied the deluge: cheap rum, loud music, dice rattling on warped tables. Wet wool steamed; salt and smoke and spilled beer moved with every slam of the door. Regulars ignored the leaks.

The door creaked open under the wind's weight.

A figure stepped in, dark clothes beneath a rain-soaked mantle, water pooling at his boots. He paused, scanning faces with sharp intent, searching for one in particular.

After a careful sweep, he moved to a corner table where four men drank.

"I knew I'd find you here," the newcomer said.

One of them grinned without getting up: "I'd know that voice anywhere. James Wrenn, you son of the devil—where've you been hiding?"

James Wrenn: former second-in-command of the *Enforcer*. Retired early after an injury made long watches unbearable, but loyalty never left him. Tyler had never replaced him and never will.

"Here to drink, or just to remind us how nice it is being paid to sit on your butt?" O'Connell teased, raising his tankard.

"You haven't changed, Quartermaster," Wrenn shot back with a thin smile. Then his tone hardened.

"Business. Another table."

O'Connell set his tankard down and rose.

"Sorry, lads. Duty calls."

He followed Wrenn to a shadowed corner, eyes flicking to the door twice before sitting. A draft moved the lantern flame; Wrenn waited for it to steady. His gaze swept the room once more, then he leaned in, sliding a folded, rain-damp scrap of paper across the table.

"There are things moving," he murmured.

"Our friend is in grave danger. The walls have ears, move carefully."

O'Connell's grin faded. He unfolded the scrap, reading it like a tavern bill, plain as could be made: *The lantern will be lit at Deadman's Hill come the twelfth chime.*

He knew the code: Tyler's signal.

No further explanation needed. He held the paper over the candle; it caught with a sharp hiss, curling into smoke.

The fiddler, having lost his tune to the door's thunder, chose another that the room knew by muscle memory.

Wrenn eased a little weight off his left leg and let the table take it. A deckhand at the next bench argued with a cooper about whether the rain would clear the river mouth by morning; neither believed the other and both liked the sound of themselves.

"Someone's watching," O'Connell said without moving his lips. Wrenn did not ask who; men who ask are the ones who look.

He let his eyes land on the hearth for the count of four, then on the reflection in a pewter plate. The watcher turned out to be a man who had no gift for watching and a larger gift for envy; Wrenn filed the face away as a man who would sell anything for a coin and a witness.

When the paper burned, its smoke climbed in a straight line for a foolish second before it found the draft and ran.

O'Connell's fingers let the last black curl fall and he blew once as if finishing a candle.

Wrenn gave a brief nod and vanished into the storm. His bad leg twinged as he went, but he moved like a man who had decided hours ago.

O'Connell drained his tankard and left moments later—only

to be met by two uniformed guards outside. The street threw rain at him sidewise; the lantern over the door swung and stuttered light on the guards' wet faces.

"Quartermaster Dylan O'Connell?"

"Who's asking?" He kept his shoulders loose, hands empty and visible.

"By order of the Governor, you and the crew of the *Enforcer* will attend a formal debrief tomorrow at nine o'clock. Mr. Edward Norton will preside. Refusal means imprisonment and court-martial."

O'Connell's eyes narrowed. "I'll try to be awake." He brushed them past into the rain.

He took back alleys until the town's edge blurred into darkness. The cave waited in the side of *Deadman's Hill*: an old training ground for close-quarters drills, narrow and perfect for secrecy.

Inside, away from the storm's howl, Tyler waited. The cave smelled of old rope and damp earth.

"Nice night you picked," O'Connell said, water dripping from his hat.

"Bloody rain has soaked me through."

"This storm will last," Tyler replied evenly.

"So, what mess drags Wrenn out of the underworld?"

"I refused their 'one last mission,'" Tyler said.

"What? No promotion?"

"Broken promises. Lies." Tyler's voice hardened.

"Do you remember Jack the Scarred?"

"Hard to forget that face," O'Connell muttered.

"He gave me proof of dealings between the Governor and pirates… not privateers, criminals. Later, Sevington and Norton ordered me to sea. I may have mentioned I know their secrets."

O'Connell froze. "Bloody hell, Captain. Been busy since we docked. Already bored of wife and children?"

Tyler's smile was faint. "On the contrary. I did it because I don't want to lose them."

"Well, you've stirred a hornets' nest. Two guards stopped me just now… Tomorrow's 'debrief' will be an interrogation. Norton will try to turn the lads against you."

"Then I need you more than ever. Can I count on you?"

"You don't have to ask. I swore an oath to my captain."

"For Sarah's sake—and the little ones—we'll keep you breathing," O'Connell added, rough but sincere.

The cave took O'Connell's voice and gave it back smaller. Tyler kept his words measured. They had planned big things in smaller rooms with worse odds, but never with so much to lose that wore his name.

Water marked time for them; it was the only clock that could be trusted when men lied.

"What about the others?" O'Connell asked.

"I did not tell anyone yet, I am not sure who I can trust" Tyler said.

"Wrenn will keep you informed. After the debrief, find out who talks. Speak only to the officers. Lay low. That's all. Dismissed."

They parted by different mouths of the hill.

Morning came without light. Clouds smothered the sky; the air felt close and heavy. Inside the Governor's residence, some forty men queued along the great hall for "debriefing."

Behind a small door at the far end, Edward Norton sat at a narrow table. Two guards flanked him; another pair stood outside.

A list of names lay before him with a neat stack of parchment and a sand shaker. His eyes moved down the list like a hunter reading spoor.

The catch was meagre. Common sailors knew little or held their tongues, but the whispers were confirmed: Tyler had met with Jack "the Scarred." Norton needed one clean thread to pull.

He dipped his quill. "Mr. Paul Davies."

The lieutenant entered and closed the door. His posture was correct, but his eyes flicked to the guards, their folded arms, the blocked exit.

"Do you know why you're here, Mr. Davies?" Norton asked, tone cordial.

"I do. Mission debriefs," Davies replied.

"Then tell me what happened when Jack the Scarred approached your captain."

"They spoke, sir."

"Yes, I know they spoke," Norton said, eyes sharpening.

"I am asking for details. One of your marines says there was an exchange: the pirate released the merchant captain; Captain Tyler released a pirate. Then Jack said he had business with your captain, and they met aboard. You chose four men to guard the cabin. Is that correct? And remember... lying to a Crown officer carries consequences."

Davies' stomach tightened. Someone had already talked. "All correct, sir. The meeting was brief."

"Odd, isn't it?" Norton's voice dripped quiet accusation.

"A Royal Navy captain negotiating with the enemy. Did Tyler explain himself to his officers afterward?"

Davies hesitated. The meeting had unsettled him; Tyler had

not been himself. But if others had spoken... He watched the sand on the paper dry.

In the hall, a bosun coughed into his sleeve; a marine checked the buckle of his belt as if buckles did anything against the Governor's ink.

Davies kept his hands still. His father had taught him that still hands read as calm even when a man is not. Norton's hands were never still, but the movements were small: a finger straightening a corner, a thumb wiping clean a speck that had not been there.

It told Davies the man found comfort in order and would break anything that would not fit.

"Your captain," Norton said mildly, "has placed you in a difficult position. I sympathize." The word *sympathize* landed on the table without sticking to anything.

Davies heard not the word, but the two guards' boots find the same stance, a habit of men drilled to mirror. A drilled room often believed itself honest because everything matched.

When he spoke of the wax seals, the memory brought back the colour, red like a cut on fresh rope, neat round impressions that did not belong in a pirate's hand. He did not say the thought aloud, he offered only the shape of it and let Norton be the man to name it.

Norton leaned in slightly, silk soft. "Several officers have expressed concern. You wouldn't want to be the only one defending a man whose fate is already decided, would you?"

His throat dried. Was Norton bluffing, or was betrayal already blooming?

"We didn't speak with him after," he said finally. "We went to our hammocks and by morning were docking."

"I see," Norton said.

"Are you aware your captain has already committed a serious offence? He let a wanted pirate go. Treated him like an envoy. We have witnesses. Confessions."

He let the words hang, then added, low and coaxing: "If you know more, the Crown will reward you. Why risk your career for a man whose loyalties… waver?"

Duty to the Crown. Duty to your captain. The old motto slid between Davies' ribs like a blade. *Facts first.*

"I noticed a change in him after that meeting," Davies said at last.

"He was distracted. O'Connell had to repeat himself. And—I saw documents on the table in front of the pirate. Folded sheets. Sealed in red wax. They looked official."

Norton's eyes glinted. He set his quill down and slid a small chit across the table, corner stamped with the Governor's seal.

"For the record," he said smoothly, "material assistance to a Crown inquiry is noted. A writ for expedited pay and shore leave. A commendation will follow."

Davies stared at the chit but kept his hands on his knees: "If this proceeds, leave my name out of it. I've given only what I can swear to."

When he finally slipped it into his coat, the paper felt heavier than coin.

"Of course," Norton lied. "Your discretion is valued." Davies rose, heavier than when he'd entered.

Outside, Cobbs and young Jenkins waited: Cobbs stone-faced, Jenkins wide-eyed.

Rain hammered Port Royal by nightfall. The harbour lay slick beneath swaying lanterns; streets emptied to hurried shadows.

That afternoon, Lieutenant Paul Davies stood beside the *Enforcer* to sign her into repair, doubts gnawing: *Have I done right? What becomes of my captain? What will others think of me?* The yard smelled of pitch and old oak.

From the corner of his eye, the harbour clerk paused mid-ledger, head tilted. Farther along the quay, a guard affected to smoke under an awning, watching the crowd instead of his pipe.

A thin boy loitered by the Watch House door, a red kerchief looped at his wrist; when Davies looked fully, the boy was gone.

The yard foreman shouted for wedges, and the sound rang under the lean-to, clean as a bell.

A barrel burst near the cooper's bench and a boy raced to gather the iron hoops as if they were treasure.

Rain smudged the chalk marks on the plank near Davies' knee; he brushed them clean and the foreman grunted thanks without looking up.

When the shoulder collided with him, Davies' hand went off its own accord to the man's elbow to steady him

"Beg your pardon, sir!" the man called loudly.

Navy half-boots, a knuckle scarred white. The man leaned close, voice a thread: "Watch is turned. Take this. Hide it. Read it where no eyes can see."

He pressed a small envelope to Davies' chest and vanished into the rain. Davies did not turn to follow; men who turned invited eyes.

He glanced down: green wax, resin-scented, stamped with a palm frond. In one motion he slid it beneath his hatband. The paper was folded in a sailor's trifold with one corner torn—a quiet token Wrenn used when a spoken word was too loud.

"All well, Lieutenant?" the harbourmaster asked, approaching with a ledger.

"All well. Just a drunk with more rum than balance," Davies replied.

"Very good. Sign here and you're free," the harbourmaster said.

"Repairs expedited by order of the Governor. Crews start today. Mr. Norton will want the logs by dusk."

Davies signed, closed the ledger, and walked off along the wet quay, the letter cool and secret above his brow. He took the long way to his sister's.

His sister met him at the door with a towel and a scold; he took both as a seaman takes orders at a gale, a habit made on crowded decks where a tumble meant a crushed hand, without argument and with his boots already on the mat.

He made the small talk a brother owes a sister, asked after the cough two streets over, nodded at the price of flour, and climbed to his room with the towel still round his shoulders so the boards would read the right story if anyone cared to read them later.

The seal was his captain's... He set his hat on the chest as if nothing were unusual, waited for a pot to clink in the kitchen, then thumbed the wax and opened the letter and read:

Lieutenant,

This comes by a friendly hand. Speak to no one of it.
If you remain true, come when the middle watch begins to the old granary steps behind St. Matthew's. Show no light.

Burn this.

He read it twice, then held it to the candle until the last ember died. Without a word, he left the house.

The letter's words were few and left no room for pride. *If you remain true...* He had thought of himself as a man who did not need to be told that sort of thing; the line cut him and then stitched him shut in the same stroke. That envelope was the smallest weight he had held that day and it pulled on him harder than all the rest.

St. Matthew's stood squat and grey at the edge of the waterfront quarter, older than most timber buildings and one of the few that weathered every storm.

Behind it, a narrow lane led to the old granary, a thick-walled storehouse once used for biscuit and rope. Steps dropped to a recessed doorway, shadowed from the street.

Davies found it empty. He waited... once, twice, thrice the length of a prayer. A slip of paper beneath a loose stone: *Patience*.

He sat on the steps, rain spattering beyond the eaves. He counted breaths in fours and let the lane tell him what it knew: a cat jumped a barrel; a watchman's pike ticked stone and then stopped.

One by one, figures emerged from the dark.

Jenkins first, he swept the lane and rooflines before stepping in, then Cobbs, heavy where Jenkins was light, finally O'Connell.

"So, we're all here," O'Connell said, voice low.

"Let's make this quick before unwanted eyes find us." He set his back to the door and his eyes to the mouth of the lane.

CHAPTER IV

Planning

Rain drummed softly on the overhang, a steady rhythm against the tense silence. The alley smelled of wet yeast from the bakehouse and the old iron of the drain. Mist lifted off the cobbles in pale breath.

A lantern two doors down burned low and steady, a good sign: no Watch lingering with nothing to do.

O'Connell stood before Cobbs, Jenkins, and Davies, his boots planted on the granary's worn stone step, shoulders loose, chin tucked. The shape of a man who had said hard things before. His voice was low but sharp.

"Now, gentlemen… you all know what happened on our last mission. What you don't know is why we're here: our captain has been betrayed by the very men we serve."

The three exchanged looks: Jenkins quick and calculating, Cobbs slow and troubled, Davies flat with disbelief, eyes widening.

"A letter from London supposedly denies the captain's promotion," O'Connell continued, laying out Tyler's account: Norton, the governor, the orders from London.

"That's why we meet tonight. Tyler has a plan. I need to know who's in."

Silence hung over the steps. Rain found the gutter and ran;

somewhere close a mule stamped and the ring of iron travelled along the stones.

At last, Cobbs spoke, voice rough as gravel. "I can't believe the Governor would go so far. He's filthy rich already... why throw in with pirates? And the worst of them?"

"Aye, Mr. Cobbs," O'Connell muttered.

"There's no end to greed." He checked the lane with a glance, counting rooflines out of habit.

"We don't know what was said in that cabin," Davies cut in, voice low.

"Beg your pardon?" O'Connell's head came up, the old scar at his knuckle whitening as his hand closed.

"You heard me," Davies snapped.

"How do we know the captain speaks true? Did you see the letter denying his promotion? Did you see these papers he claims condemn the Governor? Do you have any proof at all?"

"I don't need wax and ribbon to tell me what a man is," O'Connell shot back, stepping in close.

His breath made little clouds between the words. "Tyler's given me proof in blood for five years. Loyal to his crew and to the King. How dare you question the man who made you a lieutenant? Without him, you'd still be scrubbing decks."

"And you?" Davies turned on Jenkins and Cobbs, "Am I the only one with sense?"

"You're right to want certainty," Jenkins said carefully, hands open at his sides.

"If this came from any other man, I'd doubt it. But this is our captain. What reason would he have to lie?"

"Davies," Cobbs rumbled, "I've seen captains turn. Tyler isn't that sort." He said it like a man setting a heavy thing down where it belongs.

"How can you be so blind?" Davies flared.

"Have you forgotten what they drilled into us at the academy? Duty to the Crown. Duty to your captain. Our duty is to His Majesty. They asked for one last mission, he should have obeyed. What do you thi—"

He didn't finish. O'Connell's right fist cracked across his jaw, dropping him to the stones. The sound was a dull, private thing; even the rain seemed to pause to hear it.

Blood spattered the step; Davies rolled to a knee, spitting red, a tooth loose in his mouth.

"Enough, Davies," O'Connell said, chest heaving.

"Do not insult us with your doubts." He shook out his hand once, as if flinging the moment away.

"You make the perfect pirate, O'Connell... violence when words fail," Davies rasped, rising unsteadily.

He spat blood to the side: "Do what you want. I will not follow you."

He touched his split lip, the taste of iron stubborn on his tongue; the oath he'd sworn to Crown and captain curdled into something he didn't recognize.

As he turned, a pistol clicked. Weapons spoke where words had failed.

"Stay where you are," O'Connell ordered, barrel levelled. "You'll come with us."

"Or what?" Davies sneered. "Will you shoot me? Add 'murderer' to 'traitor'? What a fine pair you and Tyler make."

"You'll hear the truth from the captain himself. If I must put a bullet through your foot and drag you, I will."

"I've made my choice," Davies went on coldly. "My loyalty

serves a greater purpose than rebellion."

"Let him go, Quartermaster," Cobbs said quietly. "He's a free man, as are we." The words landed like ballast.

O'Connell lowered the pistol slowly, watching Davies vanish into the rain.

"I shouldn't've done that," he muttered, not to Davies but to himself.

"Did you hear that, Captain?" he called toward the granary's half-shut door.

"I did, Quartermaster." Tyler stepped from the shadows, Wrenn at his side. The lantern light took the sheen off their coats and left hard lines.

"You carried out your orders impeccably. We know who'll be licking Norton's boots."

Cobbs and Jenkins stared. "You were here all along, sir?" Jenkins asked.

"I was," Tyler said.

"I sent each of you a letter, each with different content. Only O'Connell knew I would be here. I needed to see who stood with me before revealing anything further."

He did not sound proud of the test, only certain of the need.

He clasped his hands behind his back. "Allow me to introduce my old lieutenant and closest friend, James Wrenn."

Wrenn gave a single nod.

"We leave Port Royal in two days," Tyler said. "Plan's set."

"Where to?" Jenkins asked.

"Tortuga," Wrenn said. "I have contacts there... a man named Talbot. He will sort us out, for a price."

"And how do we leave?" O'Connell asked.

"You forget I've friends here too, Quartermaster," Wrenn

added.

"Some bought, some earned."

"We take a small fisherman's boat. The *Lullaby*," Tyler said.

"Night move. That section of the dock gets less attention. Cobbs, prepare a few smoke pots in case we need a decoy."

"Aye, sir," Cobbs said, nodding.

"Wrenn will keep you informed the same way as before," Tyler went on.

"Expect a letter with the meeting point soon. Now disperse—before any unwanted eyes take an interest." They broke apart and left by different streets.

The night after the meeting – The Governor's Residence…

The storm clawed at Port Royal's windows; inside the Governor's residence, Norton worked late in his lamplit office.

The room smelled faintly of lemon oil and damp wool; the rain made the panes hum. His desk bore neat stacks of parchment, each page a thread in the noose tightening around William Tyler.

He straightened the edge of the top sheet with a thumb that had done this a thousand nights, dipped his quill, then paused at a knock on the door.

"Mr. Norton, there is someone to see you," came the servant's muffled voice.

"I am not expecting anyone," Norton replied curtly.

"It's Lieutenant Davies, sir," called a voice from beyond the door.

"I bring the Enforcer's logbook… and further information."

Norton's eyes sharpened. "Let him in. Shut the door."

Davies entered, soaked to the bone, rainwater darkening the stone floor beneath his boots. He looked like a man emptied out.

"You're miserably wet, Lieutenant," Norton observed mildly, as if being wet was a choice. "Let me set a fire. Sit. The logbook—on the table."

Davies complied silently. As flames licked up the heart, Norton poured from a crystal decanter.

"Something to warm you?" The decanter chimed once on glass; he poured narrow, like a man who rationed everything but words.

"I would gladly take it, sir," Davies said, his voice hoarse.

Norton handed him the glass, then sat opposite, legs crossed, eyes unreadable. "I was expecting the logbook yesterday, I am a little disappointed Lieutenant. You said you have more information. Our… friend in common?"

Davies took a swallow, then met Norton's gaze. "My apologies, things did not go as planned. He gathered the officers by St. Matthew's granary. We received letters from one of his agents. There were four of us."

Norton's glance flicked to the split in Davies's lip. "I presume it was not a friendly meeting."

"You could say that. I tried to make them see reason. I earned a punch for my trouble and a pistol at my back."

"Useful," Norton said softly, quill poised above fresh parchment, "Very useful."

He began writing as he spoke, the quill whispering.

"Names?"

"O'Connell, Cobbs, Jenkins," Davies said flatly.

Norton's quill danced, neat and quick.

"Consider them added to our list. They'll be watched starting tonight." He leaned back.

"Indulge me, Lieutenant. Why abandon your captain?"

Davies exhaled through his nose. "I enlisted to serve His Majesty. At the academy they taught us: Duty to the Crown first, then to one's captain. I cannot follow a man who refuses a direct order from the Admiralty."

Norton studied him a moment—jaw easy, eyes bright—then nodded, satisfied.

"Quite so. We are but servants of the greater good." His voice softened, persuasive as silk.

"I can give you purpose, Lieutenant. At once. I need a man to learn what Tyler is plotting. Do not confront him, observe. Watch his house, follow his wife if needed. Are you that man?"

Davies hesitated only briefly. "I will do my best, sir."

"Excellent." Norton smiled faintly, the smile of a predator.

"You are dismissed. I expect to hear from you soon."

Davies set down the empty glass, rose, and left. The door latch clicked soft; the sound pleased Norton, who liked things that clicked into place.

When the door clicked shut, Norton added the final strokes to his report, the ink pressed hard into the words: *...and for these reasons I request that Captain William Tyler be declared an outlaw and condemned for treason.*

He blotted it clean, then left his office, crossing the quiet residence to the Governor's private apartments. The runner in the corridor had been turned that night; his shoes made almost no sound.

Sevington was asleep. Norton slid the sealed draft beneath the door and withdrew, his work for the night done.

Somewhere beneath Port Royal – The following day...

The storm's wind howled outside, but below Port Royal, silence reigned; the thick, tired silence of stone that had heard all kinds of plans and kept them.

Norton descended the narrow passage behind the porcelain shop, torchlight flickering across damp stone.

He unlocked the final door with two keys and stepped into a long, low room: a forgotten military barracks reclaimed by the shadows.

Rough cots lined the walls; crates of supplies stacked between them. Salt damp had curled one label; the ink bled to a grey bruise.

Eric Ogdenville looked up from a cot, report in hand. Short brown hair, a neatly kept beard, and eyes that missed nothing.

"Mr. Ogdenville," Norton said smoothly. "I trust that's tomorrow's report?"

"It is," Ogdenville replied, voice level.

"The pirates are tougher than they have any right to be. If you want my best men to hit them quick, it'll cost."

"We are in no rush," Norton said, walking to the center table.

"Striking too soon invites failure. Timing is everything."

Ogdenville closed the report and sat forward. His boots were clean in a way that said he could be messy when paid and tidy when counting.

"Then you didn't come all the way down here for routine business. What's so urgent?"

Norton's tone sharpened. "Three men require strict surveillance starting tonight. Discretion is absolute."

Ogdenville raised a brow, the kind of man who measured

work first and morals later.

"Urgent work... Best hands... Call it triple."

Norton's smile didn't reach his eyes. "You know I pay on time. Bring me results and you'll have two and a half times the usual rate. If not, you'll be paid as agreed for urgency. Fair?"

Ogdenville considered the ceiling as if cost lived up there, then nodded. "Fair... for a couple of days."

"Good. Dylan O'Connell, Quartermaster. Gideon Cobbs, master gunner. Arthur Jenkins, junior officer. All of the *Enforcer*. All answering to Captain William Tyler."

"And one more thing," Norton added.

"Anyone who looks like a runner, bring him in. If it's one of mine, I'll sort it."

Ogdenville scribbled the names. "Understood. First report by noon."

"You have my thanks, Eric," Norton said, handing him a small purse heavy with coin.

"I trust you'll make yourself invisible."

"I always do," Ogdenville replied, slipping the purse away.

Norton extinguished the torch and left as silently as he'd come, carrying the smoke smell on his coat like a private signature.

Above, Port Royal slept, unaware that shadows were already gathering around Tyler and his men. The wind had eased to a whisper; rain thinned to mist. In the eerie calm of the storm's eye, every sound rang sharply.

Three heavy knocks rattled Tyler's door—then, after a pause, two more. The window cord trembled; ash in the hearth shifted and sighed. Their old boarding signal.

Tyler rose from his chair, pistol in hand, and went to the door.

"Who's there?"

"Red Iron," came the reply; the countersign from Kingston's drill-yard. Two soft taps, one back: no answer, no painter.

He opened at once. "In. Quickly."

James Wrenn stepped over the threshold, rain dripping from his mantle, hat in his hand, eyes already measuring the room for dangers it did not contain.

He wouldn't risk exposure like this without cause.

"No time to explain," Wrenn said, breath tight.

"Take what you must and send your family away. Word is they'll declare your 'treason' today. Once they seize you, defending yourself without proof will be impossible."

"What of the plan?" Tyler asked.

"We reset once you're safe." His voice was flat, made for orders in small spaces.

"I've already warned the men: hide yourselves, burn anything that names us. If you must leave a trail, make it point to the ropewalk. Let Norton chase smoke."

On the landing, Sarah stood in her nightdress, listening. A strand of hair stuck to her cheek; she did not brush it back. She and Tyler locked eyes. A silent understanding.

"I'll dress the children," she said, moving at once. From beneath the bed, she pulled a small chest already packed: coin, papers, cloaks, bread, water, a bundle of thread and needles went in after, the kind of weapon women carry.

"We'll take only what we must."

"Go with James," Tyler said. His thumb brushed the locket in his pocket, warmth against his skin. "He'll see you safe."

"And you?"

"I will be at the cave. Second bell. If I'm not there, St.

Matthew's cistern at first light. If neither, assume I'm taken."

"I'll see them settled," Wrenn said, "then I'll come back. We'll set the board again. If asked, I'm taking my sister's children to the midwife. Keep the hoods up."

Tyler tossed names, schedules, and courier lists into the brazier, leaving harmless household bills behind. The paper curled and blackened; wax snapped like fat in a pan. He strapped a small satchel: flint, line, bread, cheese, cartridges in oiled cloth.

"I'm grateful, James," he said, joining them at the hall. "I'll meet you there."

Wrenn ushered Sarah and the children out by the back, vanishing into the alley's shadow. Lizzie clutched two buttons on a string; Tom squared his shoulders as if a street were a deck.

Tyler lingered a heartbeat, then drew the door closed behind him. The house felt like a memory: hollow, still, waiting for the storm to breathe again.

The town bell tolled—three-and-three in sharp succession, the summons to gather.

Port Royal stirred like a hive. Doors unlatched; talk rose; shutters blinked awake along the lane. Shopkeepers left counters; dock crews dropped coils; fisher wives, carters, and idlers drifted to the quay.

Lieutenant Greaves mounted a crate, a broadside in his gloved hand. Printers inked blocks; clerks hammered fresh sheets to posts. Ink shone wet as fish skin.

Greaves read aloud, his voice carrying over the crowd:

BY ORDER OF HIS EXCELLENCY SIR THOMAS SEVINGTON, GOVERNOR OF PORT ROYAL

Be it known to all people that William Tyler, late Captain of His Majesty's frigate Enforcer, hath refused to obey a direct command from the Crown and is hereby suspended from his station pending further inquiry.

Let it further be known that the said William Tyler hath been observed conspiring with three officers of the Enforcer, namely Dylan O'Connell, Arthur Jenkins, and Gideon Cobbs.

Multiple witnesses attest these men have conversed with notorious pirates, in particular the malefactor called Jack 'the Scarred.'

All inhabitants are forbidden, upon pain of being deemed accomplices to treason, to aid, harbour, or abet the aforesaid people. Rewards shall be given for information leading to their apprehension.
The aforesaid men are commanded to surrender themselves within one hour of this notice.

Officers are dispatched to secure the Enforcer's books and stores as part of the ongoing investigation.

Given at Port Royal under my hand on this day,
Sir Thomas Sevington, Governor.

A murmur rippled through the crowd. Some crossed themselves; others spat; a few men said *no* under their breath and pretended they had not. Names whispered: O'Connell. Jenkins. Cobbs.

A child climbed a barrel for a better view; gulls screamed over the masts; a dog barked and then thought better of it; the bell gave one last iron stroke and fell silent.

CHAPTER V

The Curfew

Davies stood as ordered, hidden in plain sight, keeping a quiet watch over Tyler's house. Since the proclamation, the place had remained lifeless: no candlelight, no movement. The shutters kept their blank faces; the latch never lifted. Rain left a damp signature on the sill that dried and returned, dried and returned, a slow tide on wood.

He worked a discreet circuit between there and St. Matthew's, hoping to catch some sign of Tyler; so far, nothing.

He took the measure of the house the way a sailor takes the measure of a sky. A loose shutter hook on the back window; a sprig of rosemary gone dry in the pot by the door; two scuffs on the lower step where Tom dragged his heels when told to fetch water.

The little things made a map of a family that had been here yesterday and might be again tomorrow.

He felt the oath he had sworn turn over once in his chest: Crown, then captain, and settle without comfort. It was an old lesson at the academy that men liked because it fit well on a wall: an order is a rope. You hold or you fall.

Today the rope had knots where he did not expect them. He changed his rhythm each hour—once past the pump, once across the fishmonger's awning, once down the long side of the church where gulls nested under the eaves.

Davies noted these things because men gave themselves away when they forgot that other men were watching, and because the noticing kept the doubt from crowding his chest.

He had written his first report to Norton like a clean log entry, taut and spare. He had written the second the same way and did not like how it read. This was his third report to Norton, this time in person, and the substance hadn't changed.

"Sir, I'm afraid Tyler and his family are nowhere to be found," Davies said.

Norton, seated behind his desk with a cup of dark tea, looked up briefly: "How did he know?" he murmured, almost to himself.

Then, louder: "How could he possibly have known we were coming that morning? It seems our roofs are leaking, Mr. Davies... wouldn't you agree?"

Davies inclined his head. "Yes, sir." He kept his eyes on the place where the desk's edge met the blotter; an old trick to avoid looking like defiance or like fear.

"Tyler is hiding," Norton continued smoothly. "Someone is helping him from within. I want you to find out who. Now leave."

Davies saluted, turned on his heel, and withdrew. He counted doors to steady his breathing and let the wet in his collar cool his neck.

Alone again, Norton reached for the latest sheaf of Ogdenville's reports and scanned them:

Observations – Day 3

O'Connell: seen at the tavern; did not stop. Carried a sack over his shoulder. Followed to the barracks; has not left since.

Cobbs: whereabouts unknown. Last sighting: heading for the hills with a younger man.

Jenkins: last seen leaving the barracks this morning. Followed to the butcher's shop; he had not re-emerged.

"And now they're gone as well," Norton thought. He let the line sit on the desk like a coiled rope and picked another.

He rose, crossed to a high shelf, and drew down a leather-bound registry.

Flipping to a marked leaf, his forefinger traced line by line until it stopped:

James Wrenn. Former lieutenant of the Enforcer. Injured two and a half years ago; retired ashore…

Residence: Port Royal. Trades modestly with chandlers, rope-makers, and one East Quay seamstress.

Noted in dockyard ledgers speaking with errand boys and port-hands, rarely with masters.

Norton closed his eyes, arranging the pieces aloud, each thought like a chessman placed:

"Retired yet rooted in port: access to gossip without the burden of uniform. An injury that keeps him from ranging, so he uses couriers. Seen with dockyard men, not officers: intelligence from the bilges where it is freshest. His captain's man once; his captain's shadow now.

St. Matthew's Lane is quiet at the middle watch. The butcher shop could have a backroom… Cobbs walking into the hills with a 'younger man'... likely a courier or a decoy carrying nothing of worth that looks like gold."

A thin smile touched his lips.

"It's you, Mr. Wrenn. Spider at the center of a tidy little web?"

He replaced the registry, tugged the bellpull twice, and returned to his desk.

A clerk appeared in the doorway, ink on his thumb and a fold in his collar that said he'd been sleeping on the table again.

"Take down this order and deliver it to the watch captains," Norton said. His voice was precise, clipped:

"A curfew begins tonight: from sunset until sunrise. All inhabitants are to remain indoors. No exceptions save those upon the Governor's business and bearing a written pass. Any person abroad after sunset is to be arrested and examined. Double the guards at the docks; no boat is to depart without a permit signed by the Governor and countersigned by the Harbourmaster."

The clerk's pen scratched like a mouse in a sack. He bowed and vanished to carry the order, boots hurrying, breath carefully quiet in the hallway where sound carried.

Later that day, the town bell tolled: an iron knell that rolled through the lanes and out over the harbour. Lanterns winked out one by one as the Watch made their rounds; shutters slammed, patrols formed in files of four, and hooded bull's-eye lanterns cut thin blades of light across the cobbles.

A carter caught after the bell was turned toward the Watch House, protesting his fish would spoil; the smell made his case for him and did not help it. A sailor without a pass was halted at the outer stairs and sent back under threat of iron. At the docks, the guard was doubled, muskets at the shoulder, and no boat moved without paper.

Public temper soured at once. The city does not like to be told it is night. Talk of unrest simmered behind closed shutters, of fists if it came to it.

The town wore curfew badly. Doors had learned to shut fast; voices lived closer to the floorboards, a watchman's pike left little commas of water on the flags.

Norton, in his office, weighed it and dismissed it. He would risk a riot if it meant catching William Tyler. He sorted the risks into their neat stacks and pressed each stack flat under a palm.

That same day – At the Cave...

The cave smelled of damp stone and smoke, a thin haze clinging to the air from the small fire in its ring of rocks. Wrenn kept to the side of the fire where the smoke went up clean.

He had the rare gift of hearing a man's breath for truth. He did not ask O'Connell for loyalty; he watched O'Connell set his weight and knew it; he did not ask Cobbs for readiness; he watched the way Cobbs put the coil down and knew he would lift it at the right second; he did not ask Jenkins for nerve; he watched the boy's hands and knew they would not shake when the lantern came near.

Tyler spoke; Wrenn counted the room. Tyler stood before it, coat shed, shirtsleeves rolled, speaking to the men like a captain on deck.

The wind had crept back in the dark, a quiet push through the alleys. Far offshore, the swell breathed; in the harbour, the water lay slick as oil. The curfew held: shutters barred, bull's-eye lanterns hooded, patrols moving in files of four. The board was set.

"Gentlemen," Tyler said, "it is time. We move tonight."

In the cave, a new face waited: a thin-shouldered boy Wrenn had hired, the same runner seen up in the hills with Cobbs.

"This is it. There is no turning back. If anyone wants to step away, do it now; I will not judge you."

"We're with you to the end, Captain," O'Connell said, and the others nodded.

"Good. The plan, once more. Mr Cobbs, give the boy a smoke pot, short fuse. He runs it to the ropewalk and lights it. While that goes, we split into groups. Mr Jenkins, the papers... did you get them per Mr Wrenn's instructions?"

"I did, sir. Our permit names a fishing boat called *Lullaby*."

"Perfect. If you are stopped, let them stop you. Stand easy and look as if everything is in order. O'Connell goes with you," Tyler said.

"I'll keep his nerves steady," the Quartermaster said.

"Mr Cobbs, you carry the other smoke pot under your arm in a small pack, like rations. Long fuse. If trouble finds you, use it as a decoy."

"Aye, sir."

"Wrenn and I will follow. We move at full dark. If we have not boarded by first bell, you sail without us," Tyler said.

Across the quay, the nearest patrol checked: heads turning as a sour plume began to rise over the ropewalk roof.

Within a minute, the clay pot coughed a black ribbon of smoke. Tar-stink slid under the eaves; a few sparks spat, but the ring of stones held.

The sergeant was the careful sort: he did not shout fire, which would have turned the town like a plough; he did not ignore it, which would have been stupidity.

He divided his men the way you divide bread when you do not have enough: without looking at their faces, because looking at faces makes it personal. Two trotted for the smoke, one banged on a door for a bucket, the last kept the fish-market steps.

Lanterns drifted away in a line. For a slow count of fifty, the outer stairs were left to a single watchman.

Beneath the fish-market arch, O'Connell and Jenkins emerged from the butcher's trap—no skulking, no hurry. Nets over shoulders, tarred tool pouch at Jenkins's hip, the permit folded inside.

They moved with a dock man's pace and a dock man's talk: a grunt about the tide, a complaint about a spoiled line, a single laugh at nothing at all.

"Halt," a guard ordered, stepping out with two men behind him. "Your names and your business." Jenkins answered first, calm and plain:

"Nets to the Lullaby, sir. Dawn tide won't wait." He held out the folded pass. The guard read by the shielded lantern, lips moving. He looked from paper to face, back again. The seal took the light like it always did; the countersign looked comfortable where it sat.

"Who signed this?"

"Governor's office," Jenkins said, steady. "Mr. Norton's hand; seal there. Harbourmaster's countersign below."

A pause. The lantern clicked shut.

"Mind your step. Keep to the quay."

"Aye, sir," O'Connell replied, and said nothing more as they walked on. They reached the steps above *Lullaby*: a low, beamy fishing boat under tarpaulin.

Jenkins dropped his nets in the bows; O'Connell stepped aboard as if he belonged there, sliding the permit into a waxed pouch under the thwart.

Five minutes later, Cobbs appeared: broad, solid, a canvas parcel under his arm tied like salt pork. He kept his chin down, hands easy. A constable nodded; he nodded back, just another early riser with too little coin to show for it.

On the quay, he set his bundle down, coil of line on top, clay pot beneath, fuse pinched. If a patrol closed at the wrong moment, all he needed was a spark and a show stamping it out,

"Morning," he muttered to the deck,"

"Never thought I'd be glad to see your ugly face," O'Connell said under his breath.

"Feeling's mutual," Cobbs answered, deadpan, bending to sort line. His fingers moved without looking; the line fell into a quiet figure-eight like it knew the work too.

To the east, smoke thickened over the ropewalk. A Watch file trotted that way at half-run.

At the harbour mouth, *Lullaby* stirred. O'Connell and Jenkins warped her along bollard to bollard, canvas still furled. At the outer stairs, a night guard leaned down, bull's-eye lantern slitted.

"Name your boat."

"*Lullaby*," Jenkins said.

"Permit?"

O'Connell held it up, no flourish. The guard cracked the light, saw the Governor's seal gleam, grunted, and waved them on. He did not like it, but the paper was the paper. A man's job is sometimes to trust the paper and pray it does not bite him after.

They slipped past the point where the tide tugged steady and the city's lights fell behind. The oars bit water with the small round sound of good pulling: no splash, no show. O'Connell kept his shoulders low and his head still; the way a man rows when he expects questions and wants to give only answers.

The tide took a polite hand at the stern and turned them little by little. Beyond the mole, the air carried that faint metallic tang left after rain, when the night is washed clean and the iron of the world shows through. Cobbs watched the line of shore like a man reading a straight edge for a nick.

Tyler never came down the quay. He slipped through a culvert Wrenn had shown him, palms to damp stone, and found the dinghy waiting under the arch, oarlocks muffled. He paused once, listening, then pushed off. The locket was warm in his fist before he tucked it away.

Out beyond the outer mole, a red buoy rocked in the swell. Tyler let the dinghy drift there, oars shipped, breath steady. The bell tongued once when the sea lifted it; he counted the seconds to the next and found his calm in the silence between.

At the buoy he tapped the hull with his oar: two soft knocks. One answered back from *Lullaby*.

They caught her gunwale, passed up the painter, and ghosted aboard. No one said welcome. No one needed to.

"Course?" O'Connell asked, already to the oars.

"Keep the point on your lee and row a cable's length," Tyler said quietly, "Then east-by-north for a mile. Canvas only outside the roads."

"Smoke's done its work," Cobbs murmured, watching the quay shrink: "Half the Watch is sniffing the ropewalk like hounds."

"Let them," Tyler said. "We'll give them nothing to bite."

They pulled into the greyline. The wind woke, shouldering them gently as dawn bled into low clouds. Far astern, the mole-bell tolled once, then died. A tern drew a white line across the dark and then it was not there.

Jenkins touched his coat, feeling the waxed pouch with the false logbook. The pouch felt heavier than paper and lighter than sin.

Tyler looked back once at the sleeping harbour, then ahead, where open water waited, darker than the sky. "Ready," he said.

O'Connell raised the small sail, no more than a handkerchief. *Lullaby* answered, bow lifting to the swell, and slid out beyond the harbour's breath into day.

The residence bell gave two sharp pulls: a runner's summons. Lieutenant Greaves arrived in a wet cloak, breath misting from his dash.

He carried the Watch House incident book and a folded paper sealed in twine.

"Report," Norton said.

"Sir, small fire at the ropewalk wall about an hour before dawn. Contained without the bell. During the stir, a fishing boat, the *Lullaby*, put off under Permit No. 147... Governor's seal and hand, harbourmaster's countersign. People on board seemed to be four or five, hoods up. Challenged at the fish-market steps and again at the outer stairs; pass produced both times. Sergeant logged a tar-smoke blind; no pursuit ordered due to the permit."

Greaves opened the book to the inked lines. "Sergeant notes smoke likely deliberate. Suspects diversion."

Norton read, eyes ticking down the entries. Smoke, permit, departure. His mouth thinned.

"They walked the paper while the patrol split," he murmured.

"Likely, sir," Greaves admitted. He was not ashamed to say it; the better lie is the one you tell yourself, and the sergeant had not told himself any.

"Good." Norton's voice was soft as felt. "Fetch Lieutenant Davies. Now. If he sleeps, wake him. If he's unwell, carry him."

"Yes, sir."

"And listen," Norton added, tapping the permit number.

"Find which clerk cleared this through my office. Bring him quietly. Lock down the permit book. Send to Fort Charles: no small craft clears the roads after sunrise without challenge and countersignature.

Double men at the outer stairs. Post a pair along the Palisadoes. Ogdenville to watch the butcher's and the ropewalk by first light; I want whoever lit that pot and the man who told him to."

Greaves squared his shoulders. "Aye, sir."

Norton's gaze sharpened. "This was done under a proper permit. No alarms, no panic. We will answer properly."

"Yes, sir." Greaves left.

Norton laid the permit slip beside the incident book, smoothing it with two fingers as if calming a bird. He looked at the seal again and allowed himself a small appreciation for the neatness of the theft.

"Tyler," he said softly to the paper. "Neat work."

He turned to his desk, working by lamplight. The packet for London took shape: James Wrenn named outright, the curfew breach logged, the escape *under colour of a properly signed permit.* Desertion alongside treason.

Two quick knocks.

"Sir; Davies. You sent for me?"

"Enter." Davies stepped in, rain still on his coat. Norton placed the last sheet square, sanded it, set it aside.

"Your former shipmates are gone," he said evenly. "Cleared the harbour under permit. They are deserters." Davies let the word settle. Duty to the Crown. It fits cleanly now, like a blade in a sheath. The doubt did not vanish; it sat down and crossed its legs and agreed to be quiet.

"What are your orders, sir?"

"By warrant of His Excellency, I appoint you Acting Captain of His Majesty's frigate *Enforcer*, pending Admiralty confirmation," Norton said.

"Lieutenant Greaves will serve as your first."

Davies straightened. "Aye, sir." His mouth was dry, and his voice did not show it.

"You will muster a loyal crew: volunteers from the barracks and Fort Charles. Enter their names in the Watch House muster, have them sign the articles. No tavern sweepings. Present the muster book to me at noon."

"Understood, sir. Where do I refit?"

"Draw what you need from the dockyard: small arms, powder, signal flags, cordage. The yard will grumble; let them." Norton's eyes sharpened.

"The Enforcer will finish repairs soon. Do not wait. You sail within forty-eight hours aboard the Fort Charles cutter *Swift*. Sweep the coast. Speak any smack matching *Lullaby*'s cut. When the *Enforcer* is ready, transfer and continue the hunt."

"Yes, sir." Davies saw the line of it: a small fast blade first, then the heavier sword behind. He did not dislike the plan; he disliked that it made sense enough to end in blood.

"Two points more," Norton went on. "First: Greaves will take two men, quietly bring me the clerk who passed Permit No. 147. The permit book stays locked in my office. No copies, no extracts."

Davies nodded. "Understood."

"Second: rules of engagement. Within harbour I do not want any wild discharge, nor public hazard. Outside you can use force as you see fit. Your aim is to make prisoners. Tyler is to be taken alive."

Davies met his gaze. "I'll see to it, sir."

"Go," Norton said, reaching for wax and seal. "You sail on the first tide Swift can catch. Dismissed, Captain."

Davies did not ask where the line would draw blood first; he had learned that lines decide such things without asking. He thought instead of the muster book's square, blank spaces—the ones where a man signs and becomes part of a ship's will—and tried to see which hands would fill them.

Greaves would bring him good names; he liked names that could be counted on to be at the right place at the right bell. He would take them and hammer them into a crew as if he had a full forge and not a wet yard and short time.

Davies saluted, boots quick in the corridor. Norton drew the Governor's seal across the last ribbon, pressed it, and watched the wax cool. The impression lay perfect: the iron, the palm, the faithful circle of law.

CHAPTER VI

New Purpose

"You said you had a plan! Tyler was in our hands, and you let him slip away! Why do I even pay your men if they can't do half a job? I should never have entrusted you with this! We must stop him now; London cannot catch wind of our operations!"

Sevington's voice carried down the corridor like a lash in an empty hall. The door stood open; rain stitched the window beyond slant threads.

Norton did not rise to meet it. He watched the governor's colour run a shade hotter, counted the beats in his chest the way he counted a swell, and only when the breath ran short did, he choose his words with care.

"This serves us better, sir."

Sevington squinted. "And how, Edward?"

"Our packet is already away. London will not see my report for several weeks... In that window Tyler is a named deserter in a small boat with no crew to speak of.

He cannot threaten convoys or hold the roads. Lieutenant Davies sails within forty-eight hours in the cutter *Swift* and will transfer to the *Enforcer* the moment she's fit. We will sweep the coast, take prisoners, and bring them back to jail to await sentence."

Sevington's lip curled. He tapped two fingers on the chair-arm as if testing the grain. "He had better."

"He will," Norton said evenly.

"Meanwhile, we close the leaks. The permit book is locked in my office; Greaves is bringing me the clerk who passed the paper. Ogdenville has eyes on the ropewalk and the butcher's shop. The curfew holds.

We tighten, not thrash." He spoke as if laying out tools on a cloth: one, two, three, in order. Sevington leaned forward until the chain at his neck clicked.

"When you find who talked, make an example. Publicly. My authority will be respected. I will not be made a fool."

"As you direct," Norton said, already turning to the door. "But quietly until Tyler is in hand. No spectacle that spooks the quarry."

Sevington's jaw worked. "See that you're right, Edward. One more failure and I'll feed you to the sharks."

Norton bowed the smallest bow. "I will bring you results, sir." And he was gone.

Davies set two tables: one under the arch at Fort Charles, one by the barracks yard, and sent the word through the sergeants like a drumbeat.

It wasn't hard; most men had not heard the full tale, and some from the *Enforcer* came forward out of duty to the Crown. The rest came because a ship is a purpose and a ration and a clean shirt twice a week.

He took names into the Watch House muster, had each man sign the ship's articles, and turned away tavern sweepings when they tried to crowd the line.

Greaves stood six paces off with his arms folded and a way of looking that made the worst of them remember a chore they had left half-done elsewhere.

Within an hour the queues ran down the lane; within three he had his complement. A pen bled out, a fresh one scratched on. Names stacked like cordwood.

Norton's order was forty-eight hours. By the fifteenth, Davies could have sailed: the cutter *Swift* had enough hands, powder and small arms drawn, cordage and flags issued, and a first drill sketched on a slate in hard, short strokes.

It was an early signal; he could be trusted with weight and would carry it. The responsibility sat straight on his shoulders; he did not try to shrug it into comfort. He waited only for his first lieutenant. Greaves was busy bringing his suspect under Norton's eye.

"Here he is, sir," Greaves said, holding the clerk by the arm, hatless and pale. Paper ash freckled the man's sleeve.

"We found him burning correspondence when we entered his room."

Norton stood at the window a moment longer, ordering his questions, putting them in a line that would leave no gaps, then turned.

"Good. Wait outside. I'll call you when I'm done."

"As you command, sir." Greaves withdrew.

"Stand up, then sit," Norton said, indicating the chair with an open hand. He preferred to start men on their feet; it put the floor under the first lie.

"Your name?"

"M—Matthew. Matthew Elmhurst, the registry clerk, sir." The clerk's voice shook.

"You don't need be nervous, Matthew," Norton said, voice even. "Think of this as a talk among friends. If you tell me the truth, we can spare you the spectacle of a formal process."

He set a blank sheet on the desk and lifted the inkwell lid, dipped his quill, and said: "Start with this: how did permit No. 147 leave my office?"

"S-Sir, it wasn't me, I swear. I-I was only burning old registry scraps. They'd served their p-purpose," the clerk blurted, words tripping over one another.

Norton's tone stayed mild. "We do not burn registry paper without a docket order. If you have one, produce it."

Elmhurst swallowed. Nothing.

"Very well. Let us look at the books." Norton lifted a calf-bound volume from the shelf and dropped it onto the little tea table, so it thudded once.

"The Permit Day Book. Open Folio Seven. Read aloud the last entry signed by me yesterday."

Elmhurst turned pages with damp fingers. "N-No. 136... harbour victualling pass... signed at the fourth hour."

"Louder," Norton said.

"Permit No. 136, sir."

"Good." Norton tapped another paper, the Watch House incident book. "And yet the watchman at the outer stairs this morning recorded a pass shown as Permit No. 147. Between 136 and 147 sits a batch. Who moved it?"

"I-I don't know, sir."

"We'll try the registry," Norton said, drawing down a second volume and laying it open so the leather sighed.

"This is the Assignment Book. Turn to the second page and read out the duty line for yesterday."

Elmhurst read until the line snagged in his throat. "M-Matthew Elmhurst - Official Documents Registry."

"Thank you," Norton said, still courteous, and the courtesy was the most frightening thing in the room.

"That means you logged, counter-signed, and kept the counterfoils for permits issued that day. We found no counterfoils in your room, only ashes. So, I will ask you again, simply: who brought the batch to my desk for sealing, and who took it back out?"

Elmhurst's gaze flickered. "A-a clerk from the Governor's room, sir. He said you had initialed and told me to expedite. I left the bundle on your desk and he... he fetched it 'for sealing.'"

"Name."

"Mr... Hartwell, sir."

"And the runner?"

"Abel Rooke, from the east gate. He carried the pouch."

"Who ordered you to burn the counterfoils?"

"No one," Elmhurst whispered. "I panicked." Norton regarded him for a moment, measured the tremor in the throat and the sweat at the hairline, then nodded once.

"That at least is truth shaped. You will write a full account: names, hours, what you touched and when. If it holds, you will be charged with negligence rather than forgery. If it wobbles, you will hang your hope on the rope." He used the bell once. The door opened a crack.

"Greaves," Norton said, eyes still on Elmhurst.

"Quietly bring me Mr. Hartwell of the Governor's outer room and detain Abel Rooke. Seal this man's quarters and the permit book. No copies, no extracts."

"Aye, sir," came Greaves's voice, and the door shut again.

Norton set a clean sheet before Elmhurst and placed the pen.

"Write."

Within the next hour – Norton's Office...

The corridor outside had learned quiet; doors closed with a kiss instead of a clap. Greaves returned within the hour, cloak beaded with mist, two men in tow: a neat fellow with ink on his cuffs and a runner in a stained jerkin with sea-salt on the hems.

"Mr. Hartwell, Governor's room," Greaves said, releasing the neat one. "And Abel Rooke, east-gate runner. Door guard posted."

"Good," Norton said.

"Separate rooms. Rooke waits. Mr. Hartwell stays."

Greaves nodded, steered the runner away, and shut the door.

Hartwell stood straight, hat in hand, eyes flicking to the desk where the Permit Day Book lay open beside a folded slip tied with red thread.

"Sit," Norton said, and, when Hartwell did, laid the folded slip on the table between them with two fingers, as if it might sting.

"Do you recognize this hand?" Hartwell glanced once and went pale. "It looks like your initials, sir."

"It does," Norton agreed, and turned the paper so its face showed. Four words blossomed in a tidy italic: *By hand. Expedite now. E.N.*

"I have never written 'by hand' in an internal note in my life," Norton said mildly.

"I write 'under my hand,' when I write at all. And I never instruct expedites now without a docket. So let us begin again: who brought you this?"

Hartwell swallowed. "A messenger from... from the Governor's outer room, sir. I assumed—" His voice tripped on the word, and his mouth did not want to say it again.

"You assumed wrongly." Norton reached for a narrow wooden case, clicked it open, and slid out a sliver of the seal-cabinet tally: a stamped tin tag with a split bend.

"When the seal is used in my absence, this tally is checked, signed, and returned unbent. Yesterday it came back bent." He set the little tin piece down; it rocked once and settled.

Hartwell stared at the metal. "Sir, I— the note came while you were at dinner. It said the batch was to be finished to spare you the hour.

I fetched the seal from the drawer, had the wax warmed, and pressed the Governor's wafer. I believed I was acting correctly."

"Belief is not a defense" Norton said, not unkindly. He slid across the Assignment Book. "Read the duty."

Hartwell read, voice thinning. "Matthew Elmhurst - Official Documents Registry."

"Which means Elmhurst logged and countersigned the counterfoils, and you vouched the batch into and out of my room," Norton said.

"We have the watchman's line at the outer stairs: Permit No. 147 shown. We have the harbourmaster's countersignature properly placed.

We have no counterfoil and no dock in the register. And we have a runner named Rooke who probably carried a sealed pouch for you from the Governor's corridor to the harbour scribe before dawn."

Hartwell's hands tightened on his hat. "Sir, I am not... I am not bought. I was duped."

"I know," Norton said, letting him breathe a fraction. "Which is why you are in a chair; and now in custody."

Norton said *custody* like saying *coat*: a fact, not a threat.

He lifted a finger to the bellpull. Greaves stepped in at once. "Lieutenant Greaves, take Mr. Hartwell to the inner room," Norton said. "Quietly. Seal his desk and quarters. Post a man. Then bring me the runner."

"Aye, sir." Greaves took Hartwell by the arm, no fuss, no clank of irons, and ghosted him out. A minute later he returned with a lean man in a stained jerkin, salt at the hems.

"Abel Rooke, east-gate runner," Greaves said, and shut the door.

Rooke's eyes flicked to the open Permit Day Book, then to Norton's face. He had the look of a man who had learned not to be the first to speak in any room.

"Mr. Rooke," Norton said pleasantly, "you carried a sealed pouch before dawn." Rooke said nothing.

Norton turned a page in the Assignment Book with a dry whisper.

"Speak now and you walk out with coin and a badge. Keep silent and you walk out to the cells. Which suits?" He did not raise his voice; the choice grew tall all by itself.

Rooke wet his lips. "Coin, sir."

"Good. Who put the pouch in your hand?" Rooke stared at the floorboards. "A man from the Governor's corridor told me to fetch at the harbour scribe, sir." Norton waited.

Rooke looked up, met the calm, and blinked first. "The one who paid me after wasn't from the corridor. He goes by Wrenn, soft voice. Stands easy like a gentleman who's been to sea. I've carried twice for him before."

Norton did not move. "Say the name again."

"James Wrenn," Rooke said, firmer now, because coin was on the table and lies were not.

"How did he work it?" Norton asked.

"He doesn't walk far. Favors the ropewalk's lee to talk, less wind. Pays in quarter-guineas, clean coin. Uses chalk for drops: two short lines on a post means 'under the eaves in five minutes.' Keeps his hood up in the lanes.". A small cross means abort.

"Are you loyal to him?" Norton asked. Rooke snorted once. "I am only loyal to bread, sir."

"Excellent." Norton opened a drawer and set down a small purse. It made a heavy, hopeful sound.

"Here is more bread than Wrenn gives. You will go on carrying for him. You will tell Lieutenant Greaves what you carried, when, who stood where, and what was said.

You will not embroider. If Wrenn asks you to press 'by hand', you will say: under your hand, sir; Harbourmaster must see it,' and send him to the east gate.

There, Greaves will have a pair waiting." Norton watched to see if the man could repeat the phrase; Rooke mouthed it once and nodded.

Rooke eyed the purse. "And if I'm caught between you and him?"

"You won't be," Norton said. "If you bring me useful work, you keep the purse and your hide. If you try both sides for clever, you keep neither."

Rooke nodded once. "I understand."

"Good. Take your coin and go out by the side door. Greaves will show you the badge and the mark we use." Rooke pocketed the purse and went, lighter on his feet. Norton belled again. Greaves returned.

"Hartwell is held?" Norton asked.

"Sealed and settled," Greaves said.

"Now take this down," Norton said, sliding a blank sheet forward and speaking the words as he wrote.

"Order: *PURIFICATION*.

Scope: the ropewalk boys, the butcher's back room, the East Quay seamstress who passes thread and notes, the two chandlers used for small purchases, the runner posts at east gate and fish-market arch.

Actions: suspend port badges, seize notebooks and slates, detain messengers, shadow suspected handlers; no public noise, no bell.

We pull threads quietly until the net lies flat."

The word *purification* sat on the page like a blade laid on cloth.

He looked up.

"Coordinate with Ogdenville. I want names, ledgers, and one man at the center before dusk."

Greaves nodded, face set. "Understood. Quiet and clean." He checked the binding and the tie, then pressed the wax seam along the fold so the parcel lay flat and dry.

"Go…" Greaves took the folded order and was gone.

Norton set the bent tin seal-tally on the corner of the desk and touched it with a fingertip. "Your move, Mr. Wrenn," he said to the empty room.

By noon the Watch House muster was signed and the articles witnessed. New hands filed past the table at Fort Charles, each man's name set in a tight clerk's hand, each mark neat as pride could make it.

Davies closed the book, passed it to Greaves, and stepped

aboard the cutter *Swift*.

Greaves had already set the bones: watches named, stations chalked on the mast, powder chest locked and keyed to his belt. He ran them through a tacking drill in harbour air.

Hands to braces, sheets tended, helmsman answering short. No wild calls, no show; the deck learned his rhythm in seven clean turns.

Stores came aboard in measured bites: signal flags in a waxed roll, coast charts, fresh cordage, beef side, biscuit, and two spare sweeps.

Greaves checked flints and slow-match and made the young ones repeat the rule: "No sparks near powder."

Davies had the muster book brought to him once more. He set a finger under the last name, then lifted his eyes to the heads beyond the bulwark.

"You are mustered to His Majesty's service," he said, voice even. "We hunt deserters. We take prisoners. No stray shots within harbour waters." He looked at Greaves. "Cast off."

The *Swift* leaned to the tide and slid past Fort Charles with a rattle of blocks and a tug of wake.

The fort's guns loomed black and rain-wet; a sentry touched his hat and turned his face out to sea. A returning smack was hailed off the Palisadoes; the master lifted a hand and gave what he had: a stink of tar, smoke near the ropewalk before dawn, a small fishing boat easing out under a proper permit.

His mate added a time by the church bell and then remembered the curfew and closed his mouth. No names, no faces. Just the hour and the stink.

"Set your pattern," Davies said.

Greaves tapped the slate with the butt of a chalk. "Palisadoes

→ Hellshire → Old Harbour today. If nothing bites, up the coast on the morning ebb; Port Morant in sight, then a north-side run in hops. We speak every smack that matches *Lullaby*'s cut."

Davies nodded. "Make it so." He put a finger on the slate's edge to keep the plan from sliding about in his head.

The cutter took a cat-paw and shouldered into open water, flags cracking, Davies on the weather rail in a hunter's quiet, the curve of the Palisadoes falling astern.

Greaves stood by the shrouds and counted heartbeats between gusts; the pattern pleased him.

By midafternoon the *Swift* had Hellshire abeam and jogged for Old Harbour. Twice they hailed small craft and twice the answers were fish and salt and nothing else.

Davies traced their pattern on the slate and did not push beyond the plan. The hunt was in motion.

Somewhere near the coast – The Lullaby...

They kept to the lee, riding the shoreline's darker water until the sun climbed and softened the wind. Mangrove scent came and went; a frigatebird wrote a slow figure over the shallows.

By late morning Wrenn lifted a hand toward a crumple of limestone near Old Harbour Bay: a small cove with a fish-shed, two skiffs on rollers, and, under a sun-faded tarp, a coastal sloop no bigger than a town house, her mast stepped, her sheets coiled clean.

"Quiet notch," Wrenn said. "Owner sleeps ashore. Good lines. Newer cordage." He spoke like a man ticking off virtues in a potential friend.

They let the *Lullaby* drift to the mangroves and hooked a root.

O'Connell and Jenkins went first, soft-footed over the stones. Cobbs followed with a coil and a knife for old lashings.

Up close the sloop showed careful hands: plugs tight, bilge sweet, a tidy locker of spare cleats. O'Connell slipped the tarp, eyes flicking to seams and cleats and places where good owners cheat and bad ones forget. "She'll answer," he murmured.

"Name?" Tyler asked.

"*Sea Fern*," Jenkins said, reading the faded paint on the transom.

"Good omen or a liar," Cobbs said dryly, easing the halyard free.

They moved with a dock man's economy: Jenkins checked the mast wedges, Cobbs bent a single reef into the main with square, patient hands, O'Connell ran the sheets and found the sculls.

Wrenn set a small purse and a folded note under the companionway board:

Requisitioned in emergency. Hull to be returned or paid. No damage intended.

Four clean coins lay in a square on top. Honest weight. He was careful with the corners; honesty reads better when the paper is neat.

"Hide our old skin," Tyler said. They walked the *Lullaby* deeper under the mangroves, tied her off low, and threw a net and two palm fronds over her bow.

A crab lifted a claw at them and thought better of it. The false logbook was left beneath the thwart in its waxed pouch; insurance of a kind if she was found.

"Lines off," Tyler said. The *Sea Fern* lifted her head to the little breeze as if pleased to be asked. O'Connell eased the sheet; the boom crept, the sloop gathered way and nosed past the fish-shed with hardly a wrinkle. No one came to the door.

"Keep her dull," Wrenn said. "No flourish." Boring boats live long.

They slid out to the point. The reef there lay like a cat's back, white in patches; Jenkins called the water, Cobbs nudged her with the scull when she hesitated. Past the last pale patch, the sea darkened and opened. "Course?" O'Connell asked.

"Keep the coast under your lee until the sun falls," Tyler said.

"When night comes, we slide out for Tortuga." He did not look at anyone when he said the name; the wind took it and made no comment.

Wrenn stood a moment, eyes on the weather. "If anyone asks, we're *Sea Fern* out of Annotto Bay with nets to mend. And we are boring."

"Boring," Tyler agreed. He set a hand to the tiller and felt the sloop answer; steady, honest, eager enough.

Behind them, the cove shrank to a fold in the rock and then to nothing a man on shore would notice if he were not looking hard.

Ahead, the south coast ran away in a green line and beyond it the darker line of open water, the road to where Jack the Scarred drank and Talbot dealt.

"Ready," Tyler said. He touched the locket once under his shirt and let go.

O'Connell raised a handkerchief of headsail. *Sea Fern* leaned, took the breath of the trades, and slid east-by-north, bowsprit lifting to the swell: toward Tortuga.

CHAPTER VII

Tortuga

The storm was long gone. Heat lay on Tortuga like a forge-lid, the water brassy under a pitiless sun. Four dawns after their change of hull brought Tyler and his cut-down crew to the island's lee.

Tortuga was no English port. A French governor held it; an English stranger should not expect courtesy from cutters or customs men. They worked the *Sea Fern* into a derelict privateers' quay—weed on the piles, rings still sound—snugged her down and paid a dockside boy two coppers to keep an eye while they were ashore.

"Cycle back every hour," Tyler said.

"I'll make the first turn now," Jenkins answered, peeling away.

They kept to back lanes and alleyways. Even in daylight you felt what Tortuga had been: a town raised on plunder and prize courts. A pair of Compagnies Franches drifted through a square like cats with muskets; faces turned and then away.

"Lose the hoods," Wrenn murmured without looking at them.

"Nothing says outsider like a hood in daylight." Stepping off the curb, he hid the stiffness in his bad leg; the old wound still spoke in damp heat.

O'Connell grunted but shoved his back. Cobbs did the same. The street seemed to breathe easier.

The tavern they found was crowded and foul in a way the Old Lord never managed. Men danced on tables, the air was thick with sour beer, piss, and smoke. Shouts tangled with a fiddler sawing for his supper. Drunk pirates pawed at the maids and argued over dice.

"Where do we sit?" Jenkins asked, low, rejoining them at the door.

"We don't," Cobbs said.

"Beer first," O'Connell muttered. "Then we pick another hole."

They shouldered to the bar. Every step drew looks, but without the hoods they were only four more dock men with sunburn and bad tempers.

"Captain… one?" O'Connell said, forearm along the stained plank.

"You know I don't drink on duty, Quartermaster," Tyler said.

"Right." O'Connell tipped his chin at the barman. "Two beers."

The barman slammed down pewter. O'Connell slid a silver under his own mug with two fingers and didn't look at it again.

"We're after a man who keeps ledgers straight," he said, easy as rope. "Name of Talbot. Quiet talk, no fuss."

The barman didn't blink. He palmed the coin and wiped the same spot twice.

"La Sirène," he said at last. "Upstairs gallery after dusk. Ask for anisette, don't drink it. That tells Talbot you're waiting."

"Obliged," O'Connell said.

The fiddler scraped another tune. Somewhere behind them a

chair went over, and a laugh turned mean. They stood like men waiting for their change, and the tavern forgot them.

Two days earlier - South Coast, near Old Harbour Bay...

Captain Davies kept the cutter outside the shoals, working a zigzag where the water held its darker colour. Boats went into the shallows; smacks and fishers were boarded; names logged without temper.

By mid-forenoon a narrow canoe flitted under *Swift*'s quarter.

"Pardon, sirs—are you Navy?" the man called up.

"We are. Captain Davies. Your business?"

"My boat was stolen yesterday," the man said, holding up a folded paper. "Whoever took her left this."

"Bring him aboard," Davies said. "Side ladder; steady there!" Hands helped the fisherman over. He set the paper and three coins in Davies' palm.

Davies read: *Requisitioned in emergency. No damage intended.* Four clean words, an honest square of coin. "Name of your boat?"

"*Sea Fern*, sir. Out of Annotto Bay."

Davies glanced at his first lieutenant. "Lieutenant Greaves; take this man's particulars. Note the cut of his sloop: mast, canvas, any marks."

"Aye, sir," Greaves said, already reaching for the slate.

"And raise a search notice," Davies added. "Description of the *Sea Fern* to all watch houses and harbour posts along this stretch. Speak every sloop that matches."

"Aye."

Davies turned back to the fisherman. "Where was she

berthed when she went missing?"

"In a little cove, mangroves thick as broom," the man said, pointing. "Two points east."

"Launch a boat," Davies said. "Six hands. Sweep the mangroves."

Twenty minutes later came a hail from the green tangle: "Boat here, sir!"

Davies himself went in the second boat, oars whispering through brown water. They nosed into a dark pocket under the roots. There she lay: a fishing boat shrouded with net and palm fronds, her name just visible on the worn transom... the *Lullaby*.

"Strip the cover," Davies said.

A hand lifted the net; another reached beneath the thwart and came up with a waxed pouch. Greaves opened it carefully: a logbook—neat, innocuous.

"Papers," Davies said, satisfied. "Bring her out."

They warped the *Lullaby* into the light, secured her astern of the *Swift*. Davies looked down the line of coast toward Port Royal. "We've what we came for. Hands to stations! Set course for Port Royal. Greaves; mark the position and send the *Sea Fern* description ahead with the first rider ashore."

"Aye, sir."

The cutter gathered way, the *Lullaby* tugging dutifully in her wake, and Davies laid a hand on the recovered logbook.

"I will make you answer for your crimes," he said under his breath. "One at a time."

Back in Port Royal...

Grey dawn found the *Swift* sliding past Fort Charles with the

Lullaby trotting astern on a short painter. The curfew bell had died hours before; the harbour lay flat and watchful. Greaves sent a boy up to the Watch House with the note and four coins, logged the tow on the quarterdeck slate, and hailed the quay.

By the time they warped alongside, a yard gang stood ready to haul the recovered boat under guard, and Davies was already taking the steps two at a time toward the Governor's offices; paper in his pocket, course-lines in his head narrowing to one name: *Sea Fern*.

"Sir, we found the *Lullaby*, and this note," Davies reported to Norton, who was sipping his morning tea.

"They've traded up to a better sloop. My read is they're still working these waters... for now."

"Very well, Captain. Log the note and coins as evidence, search the *Lullaby*, then return her to her owner," Norton said.

He glanced at the door. "And have scribe Chard copy the note-and coin entry into the Permit Day Book as a cross-reference. I want the paper trail tight."

"Right away, sir," came a voice from the threshold.

"One last thing before you go: the *Enforcer* is fully repaired. Speak to the Harbourmaster, Mr. Tobias Keane, and begin provisioning. Sail as soon as you're fit. Do you have a heading?"

"Understood, sir. We're plotting sweeps along the south coast. We've posted descriptions to the Watch Houses to report any sighting of a sloop answering to the *Sea Fern*'s description."

"Good, Mr. Davies. Dismissed." Davies saluted and left.

On the harbour the work was a din of hammers and shouted numbers; carpenters shouldered long planks; caulkers moved like ants along the seams.

"Excuse me," Davies asked a yard hand. "Looking for Mr.

Keane."

"You'll find him by the office, Dock Four."

The Harbourmaster was at his desk, pen scratching.

"Captain Davies," Keane said, looking up with a brief smile. "Last time I saw you, you were still a lieutenant. Congratulations on the step."

"Thank you, Mr. Keane. I was as surprised as anyone."

"Here for the *Enforcer*, then?"

"I am."

Keane turned to a muddle of folders that somehow obeyed his hand. "Not this... nor this... ah." He tugged free a sheaf.

"Here we are—your logbook and the repairs list. She'll shift berth tomorrow, but you can start provisioning at once; she's in Dock Two."

"Very good. My thanks."

"Captain... before you go." Keane lifted a small, leather-bound book.

"Found it during the sweep of the great cabin. Might interest you."

Davies took Tyler's personal log, thumb running over a water-stained spine and the torn ribbon that hung from it. He weighed it without opening. "It does. Thank you."

He slipped it inside his coat and stepped back into the noise of the docks. Alone a minute later under the lee of a shed, he opened to a page scrawled in a firmer hand, Sarah and the children named in a margin, and shut it again as if it had burned, the book heavier for it.

The next morning the mixed company—old hands and new—filed aboard the frigate. Davies stood by the quarterdeck rail.

"Gentlemen," he said, clear and even.

"For some of you this deck holds memories; for others, it will make them. Our charge is simple: four men deserted His Majesty's service, abetted by a fourth whose loyalty failed. We will find them. We will take them into custody. We will keep our discipline, and we will keep the King's peace while we do it."

A growl of approval ran the length of the deck.

"Mr. Greaves; make the ship ready for sea."

"Aye, sir." Greaves turned sharp. "Hands to the capstan! Cast off the warps! Loose fore and main; hands to braces!"

Blocks rattled; canvas bellied. The frigate leaned to her work.

"Quartermaster Simmons," Davies called, "take the wheel. East-by-north for Morant Point. We'll go round the point and work up along the north coast by evening. We ask every coaster and fishing smack for a sloop answering to *Sea Fern*... hull low, paint worn on the transom."

"Aye Captain; East-by-north," Simmons answered, easing the spokes.

"Signal book to hand," Davies added, quiet to Greaves. "No stray shots in harbour waters. Remember: we hunt clean."

Tortuga present day - La Sirène...

The upstairs gallery at La Sirène ran like a crooked horseshoe above the main room: plank floor scoured with salt, a low rail, little tables in shadow. Lamps were turned down to rims; smoke drifted and hung.

Below, the fiddle sawed on and dice clacked; a girl laughed, too bright to be happy. A *garçon* slid past with a muttered "*pardon, messieurs,*" and a girl laughed "*bon soir*" at a purse with quick fingers.

They took a table with a view of the stairs. O'Connell stood two paces off at the rail like a man cooling his drink; Cobbs faded into a corner where a pillar swallowed half his width.

Wrenn lifted a finger, and a boy came with a tray and a bottle that smelt of liquorice and fire.

O'Connell scanned the room on a slow pivot, marking who wore steel, who watched the door, and who watched them.

"Anisette," Wrenn said. "Leave the bottle." They poured one glass and did not touch it. It took less than a minute.

A wide man in a pale linen coat came up the stairs as if the steps were his. Soft belly under the coat, thick wrists, rings that had seen more ledgers than rope.

His hair was pulled into rope-thick locks, bound back at the nape with a red kerchief: sun and salt had burnished them as much as his skin. The face said Kingston before he opened his mouth: broad, steady, amused; yet he carried himself like an officer who had learned not to care who saluted.

He stopped a pace short of the table, eyes on the untouched glass, then on Tyler.

"Captain Tyler," he said in good English with a French bite over Kingston vowels, pleased to say the name correctly. "And Mr. Wrenn. You took your time."

"Talbot," Wrenn said. "You look fed."

"Better than when we last did business," the man said, smiling with only half his face.

"Back then you wore a uniform, and I had a letter of marque. These days I keep ledgers and introduce people who ought to talk. Sit easy. If the Compagnies come in here it's to drink, not to count."

Tyler inclined his head. "We need three things. A crew, a hull that will live outside a roadstead, and to speak with Jack the Scarred."

Talbot waited until a girl set a clean glass at his elbow. He didn't touch it: "No small shopping list, but I was prepared. James kept me informed. The crew I can muster in a night, if you don't mind hands with mixed flags. The hull? It costs more. As for Jack..." He let it trail, as if the name itself had a price. "You brought coin?"

"Not enough," Wrenn said. "But not empty."

Talbot's eyes narrowed—amused rather than sharp. "Then how did you come here?"

"A small sloop," Tyler said.

Talbot's glance flicked to O'Connell and back. "Where?"

"Old privateers' quay," Wrenn said. "Rings still sound."

"That will do as a first bite," Talbot said, as if discussing fruit. "Down payment. Your berth tally and a brief handover note will do. I'll have her warped out by dusk."

He tipped a finger toward the anisette. "You can follow instructions. Good. But you still owe."

"We'll square the owned when we can," O'Connell said under his breath.

"We know," Tyler said. "We're not here to buy comfort. We're here because we hunt papers... official ones. We want a hull and a crew to move fast; we want Jack because he showed me what I needed to see once, and he can do it again. We'll take documents before coin, and we don't spill blood to get them."

Talbot's eyebrow ticked. "You hunt documents."

"We do," said Wrenn. "Bills, ledgers, sealed letters; the sort that go missing when men need them most."

Talbot considered; then he sat. He turned the anisette glass a fraction—ritual more than thirst.

"Three offers," he said. "First: a tired brigantine called *Marigold* that a Saint-Domingue planter wants gone. Her knees are sound; she needs canvas and tar and men who don't mind a pump-handle. I can get you the title clean enough for Tortuga."

"Second?" Tyler asked.

"A dead-claim sloop, the *Saint-Jude*, lying just outside the roadstead. Jury-rigged and riding a rotten buoy. She was cut loose after a quarrel over shares. Nobody's had the stomach to settle it with the men involved. No killing," Talbot added, lazy as a cat. "Just a removal. Look like you mean it and they'll run."

"And the third?"

"You charter under my bond for a month. I put you on a brig with a captain who keeps his eyes forward and his hands out of your pockets."

Tyler didn't look at Wrenn and Wrenn didn't look at Tyler. O'Connell shifted his weight by the rail; below, a laugh tipped toward a fight and stopped.

"And Jack?" Wrenn asked.

"You get Jack's Quartermaster tomorrow at noon at the fish quay," Talbot said.

"Jack doesn't walk into rooms like this. If you don't foul my island in the process, you get Jack the day after; on a beach where a man can see who's coming."

"And the crew?" Tyler said.

"Twenty by dawn if you don't ask origins. Thirty if you shake some coin loose." He glanced at the untouched glass. "Drink that or leave it. Either way, don't break the glass."

Tyler stood. "We'll take the third. Charter under your bond. Our sloop is yours as deposit."

Talbot rose with him, quietly. "Then come to Dock C at first light." He turned, already someone else's shadow.

Wrenn let a breath go. "He's the same as ever."

"Useful," Tyler said. "And expensive."

"Thank you," Tyler added, offering his hand.

Talbot took it; dry, brief. "Don't thank me. This isn't charity. Payment is expected in full. I'll tell you tomorrow what else I need to call the debt paid. If it doesn't arrive, there will be consequences."

Tyler nodded once. "We're aware."

"Beds for the night?"

"We've coin enough," Tyler said.

"Good. Dock C at first light."

He went... pale linen slipping into smoke. The gallery breathed again; below, the tavern's noise rolled on. Outside, runners peeled off the quay, and the pieces on the board began to move.

The next morning - Dock C...

Dock C woke in smells: tar, bilge, cut rope, the cold iron of anchors.

Talbot was already there, pale linen open, red kerchief at his nape. He looked like a man who had slept three hours and didn't mind it. Two of his men stood behind him with the posture of paid calm.

"On time," he said. "Good."

Wrenn set a folded registry slip on a bollard and laid a berth tally atop it—dock man's scrawl: Old Privateers' Quay. "Down payment," he said. "Painter is coiled on the rings."

Talbot touched the papers as if weighing them. "She'll be off those rings by dusk." He flicked two fingers; one of his men peeled away, whistling for a boat.

"You said a hull and a captain," Tyler said.

Talbot turned, and they followed him to a berth where a lean brigantine lay with a working beast's patience. Honest lines; paint wearing thin; deck swept; pump handles lashed, ready. A man in a dark coat stood by the mainmast with his hat in his hands.

"Captain Elijah Pike," Talbot said. "My most trusted. Honest… for his kind."

Pike nodded once to Tyler, once to Wrenn. Weather had carved him: iron-grey hair, thick knuckles.

"We can keep thirty men fed and two dozen at work when needed. She answers well. Charter is a month under Talbot's bond. You act as supercargo: your cargo is time and direction. I keep papers and sea-room."

"How about teeth?" Cobbs asked. "In case we need to speak loud."

"Six fours a side and a pair of swivels," Pike said. "They won't break a fort, but they'll break a man's nerve if you place them." Cobbs ran a thumb along a gun-carriage trunnion.

"Swap these wedges and she'll run sweeter. I'll lay slow-match and keep tubs wet."

Tyler gave a single nod. "That suits us. We'll hunt mail and light merchants and leave the Navy to its dinners."

Pike's voice stayed even. "If you drag me into a fight with the Navy, I'll hang you by the guts."

"I'll set you on the right course," O'Connell said.

"And we need hands," Jenkins added.

"Follow me," Talbot said.

He led them into a small dock-house. Twenty-three men stood there already: French, English, Kreyol, Dutch; a quiet Spaniard.

Some had tar on their cuffs; some had knives on their belts; all looked like men who'd hire on for a month and wouldn't be owned.

"These are what I could gather," Talbot said. "Twenty-three bodies. They'll work if you point them."

Tyler stepped onto a barrel. "Gentlemen," he said, voice carrying. "We sail soon. We work the Passage lanes. We do not kill unless we must save our own skins. We do not raid; we take enough to pay for your shares and to live. Our treasure is paper… anything under a red Royal seal. You may carry a pistol and a knife. If you don't like those rules, walk now. If you stay, they are your morning prayer."

No one left.

"Names at the door," O'Connell said. "Bring your kit and you see coin up front."

"Good," Talbot said. "Now we talk outside."

They stepped into the light while the new men filed their marks.

"My part's done," Talbot said. "Jack is up to you. He'll know you owe me, so don't ask for the world. To settle the debt, I want something very specific."

He took a sealed note from his coat and handed it to Wrenn. "There's a ship runs north-east every fortnight. Inside you've got courses and hours for the next month, your window. In the captain's cabin there's a small library. Third shelf down: a brown book with *H.J.K.* cut into the spine. Don't open it. Bring it to me.

Then we're square."

Tyler weighed it, then nodded. "Understood."

"Good. And remember... fish quay at noon. Jack's man doesn't like to wait."

He tipped his head, listening to some other bargain only he could hear, and left as he came. Quietly.

"I hope this 'book' doesn't buy us our first broadside," O'Connell muttered.

"We'll try words first," Tyler said. "If that fails, we'll make them blink; nothing more."

"Aye," said the Quartermaster.

"For the meet," Tyler added, "Wrenn and I go forward. O'Connell, Cobbs, Jenkins—hang back and keep eyes."

They nodded and split, one eye on the sun and the other on the fish quay. The day had work in it.

"Jenkins," Tyler added, "give Jack's Quartermaster thirty paces' lead. Mark if any shadows hang on him. Then break left. No bravado."

Jenkins nodded once, already choosing alleys in his head.

That afternoon — The fish quay

The wind pushed sand in shifting lines; palms bent and clicked. Between two squat stones a half-buried barrel sat like a rough table with rougher chairs. Men who didn't want names met here.

Tyler and Wrenn walked to it. The others—O'Connell, Cobbs, Jenkins—stayed under the trees and watched.

They didn't wait long. Three figures slid out from behind a shoulder of rock and came up to the makeshift table.

The one in the middle wore a black neckcloth and gold hoops; he was slight, but the kind of slight that never had to speak twice.

"Talbot says you want to meet the captain," he said, eyes moving between Wrenn and Tyler.

"Yes," Tyler said. "Your captain and I spoke not long ago. I want to speak to him again."

The man tilted his head. "Jack thinks you bring problems with you. Is that true?"

"Trouble follows me," Tyler said. "Yes."

"That's not good, Captain Tyler," the man said, letting the title taste sour. "It compromises the security of my captain. And he likes his privacy."

"You know my name," Tyler said. "I didn't catch yours."

The man's smile didn't reach his eyes. "I am Jack's Quartermaster; my name is not important. You're still Navy to me. You're playing a dangerous game, Mr. Captain."

"A game I must play," Tyler said, firm. "Or die trying."

The Quartermaster gave a short laugh and cut a glance at his men. "Well, well. guts like cable, Mr. Captain."

Then, business: "I don't trust you, and I don't like you. But my captain wants to hear what you have to say. I'm here to give you a time and a place."

He pulled a scribbled paper from his worn green leather coat and handed it over. He pointed up the slope at the little church that cut the sky. "Tonight, after the church goes dark."

Tyler unfolded the note. The hand was rough but legible:

From the barber shop, 30 steps left, look right.
50 steps ahead until you see the lion's mouth.

Look left again.
27 steps right until you see the blossomed roses.
Behind them there's a door.
Knock twice, each knock ten seconds apart.

Tyler read it twice; the cadence of countersigns—Navy habits wearing a pirate's coat.

"Someone at the door will ask you a question," the Quartermaster said. "You reply: 'I did not know it was his birthday.'"

"Thank you," Tyler said. "We'll meet you there tonight."

"If I were you," the Quartermaster said, turning away, "I'd pray he spares your life."

They went the way they'd come.

"That went well," Wrenn said once they were alone. "Are you sure about this, William?"

"I don't know, James," Tyler said. "I hope my instinct won't fail me."

"What business do you have with him, anyway?" Wrenn asked as they headed back to the trees where the others waited.

"He knows where to hit the Crown," Tyler said. "I want to know it too."

CHAPTER VIII

Trust and Truth

They reached the barber's shop, the shutters drawn, the street quiet save for a dog nosing the gutter.

Tyler stopped, turned to the others. "I go on from here," he said. "You wait by this shop. If I am not back by dusk, consider me taken."

O'Connell started to protest, but Tyler raised a hand. "No. This is my step to take."

Wrenn gave a short nod. The rest held their silence, eyes hard in the half-light.

Tyler drew a breath, then walked the cadence laid out in the note: thirty steps, the lion's mouth, the roses. At the door he set his knuckles and knocked twice, each knock ten heartbeats apart.

The pause on the far side was long enough to measure a man's life. Then a bolt scraped, and a voice said:

"Did you bring something for the child?"

"I did not know it was his birthday." Said Tyler

"Inside" said the voice opening the door.

The bald man lifted a shuttered horn lantern from the wall sconce and started down the steps. The stairs turned twice; the air grew damp and heavy as they went.

At the bottom, another door. He took a bunch of keys on a

bronze ring, chose one by feel, and turned the lock.

Beyond lay a narrow canal and a skiff nosed to a stone lip.

"Get on," the man said: gatekeeper, not host.

Tyler stepped in; the gatekeeper followed and rowed. The oars dipped without a splash. After five slow minutes they slid into a pocket of stone: a mini-dock, three steps, another door. Same keys; another bite of iron and wood.

Up again—short, steep—then a third door.

Inside: a small room lit by three candles. A rough wooden table; three chairs; a single musket on pegs; and, under the table, a neat coil of tarred line.

A scoured bucket sat in the corner; one knot on the tabletop was dark browned with old stain. Parlor, or cell; depending on how the talk went.

In the middle chair sat Jack the Scarred, arms folded, boots catching the table's edge. To his left, the Quartermaster; when he glanced over, silver teeth flashed. To Jack's right, another officer with a face like weathered rope.

The gatekeeper slipped back through the door and closed it behind him.

"He came," the officer said, low to the Quartermaster. "I won the bet."

The Quartermaster looked at him and showed silver again for a second.

Jack didn't rise. "Look what the sea brought me," he said, amused. "I thought I'd never see the day."

"I can't say I imagined it either, a month ago," Tyler replied.

"You have powerful friends, Captain," Jack said, blade-light. "Getting Talbot's help, a boat as deposit and a promise, is not something he does for everyone."

Tyler said nothing; weighed the wording, tested the fence.

"So," Jack went on, lazy as a cat. "A pirate and William Tyler, once the Crown's blade, now a deserter. What can I do for you, Mr. Captain?"

"You warned me that day," Tyler said.

"I kept a little hope what you showed me wasn't true. Then, when I was close to time with my family, they asked for more. That's when I opened my eyes."

Jack nodded once and steepled his hands under his mouth.

"You seem to know plenty; how they operate, names, routes," Tyler said. "I want in. I want to bring them to justice and clear my name."

"Sit," Jack said.

Tyler sat.

"Not refusing like last time," Jack observed. "Funny how things change when you've lost what you fought for." His tone cooled.

"Let's be plain: you come here with a thin crew, no ship to call yours, in debt to one of the most powerful men in Tortuga, and with the Navy likely hunting you already. Being near you is dangerous. And you ask me to open my books? You've got courage, Tyler."

"I know my position isn't the best," Tyler said, even.

"I came for an agreement. Do you know anything about a ship called the *Valiant*?"

Jack's eyes brightened a shade. "I do. Everyone is looking. Put a ship of the line under any flag out here and British, French, Spanish frigates rethink their patrols. Why does she matter to you?"

"Because I want her for myself… if she's intact."

Laughter broke from Jack and both officers: loud, honest.

"And how will you fight the rest of the dogs sniffing after her?" Jack said, wiping a tear. "With words?"

The Quartermaster leaned in, contempt easy as breathing. "Navy prayers won't float you here, Mr. Captain."

Tyler didn't blink. "Words move men; men move ships."

Jack held his stare for two beats, then straightened.

"Interesting theory. I'm almost tempted to see what you'll do with it." A beat. "But you'll have to do more to convince me. Where are your men?"

"At the barber's shop," Tyler said.

Jack flicked two fingers to his right-hand officer. "Go meet his people. Tell them their captain is willing to spend the night here. We have a lot to discuss." He turned back to Tyler.

"I hope what you have in mind interests me. Otherwise, you won't make it out of here alive." Tyler took it without a blink.

"Give me a strip of cloth or a piece of paper. I'll fold it and send it with your man. They'll know I'm well."

Jack nodded. The officer passed a small square; Tyler folded it into a sailor's trifold with one corner torn, handed it back, and the officer slipped out.

"Quartermaster," Jack said, eyes still on Tyler, "fetch us something to drink. This will be a long night."

"Yes, Captain." The Quartermaster rose and left.

Silence sat heavy. The musket on pegs, the coil of line, the brown knot in the wood; all seemed to listen.

"Ask me your questions," Tyler said at last.

"There's no rush," Jack replied. "You're my guest." He tipped his head toward the ceiling. "

Upstairs there's a tidy bar."

The latch clicked. The Quartermaster came back with a green onion-glass bottle of dark Irish usquebaugh, wax-sealed, and two small tumblers.

He set both down and poured equal measures. Without looking, Jack slid the glasses past each other with a lazy finger—an old habit of men who expect poison—then lifted the one that had been meant for Tyler.

Jack's Quartermaster hovered the bottle to top him up. Tyler set his palm over the rim. "Not for me, thanks."

He'd already clocked the make—too fine for common stock: smuggled.

Jack tasted, let the spirit sit, then threw back the rest and poured again.

"All right, William," he said.

"Start from the beginning. Don't leave any details. Let's say I allow you into my operation: then what?"

"I sail one month under Talbot's bond," Tyler said.

"Crew's a decent size. We depart in two days. I'll secure his payment in the first week; the next three I spend in the Passage. His bond helps me avoid trouble I don't need."

He held Jack's eye. "Before I tell you the rest, I need what you know about the ship and her crew. That will change my answer."

"A small piece of truth for a small piece of trust," Jack said, draining the second glass and pouring a third.

He struck a spill for his pipe and drew it alight. "Is that your bargain, William?"

"It is."

Jack smoked, then said, "If I tell you the ship was caught in dense fog, lost her reckoning, and could be anywhere inside six days of sail, what then?"

"Then we patrol that area for two weeks before we call it," Tyler said.

"That leaves you a week of safe sail, if you're lucky. What then?"

"If you share where you find the documents, we use that week to hit as many targets as we can. We don't kill unless forced, so don't expect that from me or my men. We bring you what interests you; we keep what interests us."

Jack's gaze cooled. "At the end of that week, if not earlier, you'll be without a ship and without a crew. You won't offer me anything else, because you won't be able to hunt my targets."

He leaned in, voice soft as a blade. "So let me ask you a familiar question: give me one good reason I shouldn't put a bullet in you right now."

Tyler didn't move. "Same reason as last time: I'm more useful breathing. And because I have something else you want."

Jack's mouth creased. "Which is?"

"I may be a deserter. I won't be a Commodore you can call favors from. But I've been in the Navy for fifteen years. I know routes, how they move, how they think, their watches." A dry edge.

"I even know what they're going to eat and when."

"And you, William Tyler, would give that to me—a pirate—while you're trying to clear your name with the Crown?"

"My only interest is a home on land, with my family," Tyler said.

"To get that, I must expose what was done to me, and the shadow trade Sevington and Norton run out of Port Royal. If that means giving up a few tricks, I will."

Jack watched him over the rim of the glass, the room quiet

enough to hear oil tick in the candle cups.

Jack tipped his glass once and set it down. "Very well, William, let's play. Pay Talbot's debt and prove you can live by your no-blood creed. When I hear the debt is paid, my Quartermaster will find you. Then I decide if we collaborate." His mouth thinned.

"If you're still breathing. And your rule… no blood? We'll see how the sea feels about that."

Tyler rose. "I'll see you within a week, Jack."

"Or I'll see your wreck," Jack said, almost amiable. "Farewell."

The latch clicked; the gatekeeper's horn lantern bloomed, and Tyler went back the way he'd come. The skiff slid soundlessly along the black water; keys turned; stale air gave way to night.

Up top, a shape kept pace two corners back: the Quartermaster, not hurrying, not hiding, just a shadow that knew the streets better than the sun.

By the time the church's first bell shivered the dark, Tyler stepped out near the barbers. Wind ran across the alley like a narrow river.

O'Connell stood with his back to the doorframe, the sailor's trifold with one corner torn in his hand.

"You got it," Tyler said.

"We did," O'Connell answered, low. "And we waited."

Tyler nodded once. "We have work to do."

He glanced past him: just a quiet alley and the faint salt reek of day beginning.

The token vanished into O'Connell's coat, and the crew moved off the street before the light could find them.

They slipped through back lanes to a small room Wrenn had borrowed above a cooper's yard. The place smelled of pitch and damp wood. A single window looked toward Dock C.

"Close enough to watch, far enough not to be watched," Wrenn said.

They sat around a rough table. Wrenn laid out Talbot's sealed note: red wax pressed flat with a thumb.

He cracked it and read the tight hand slowly, so they all heard it the same: "Course and hours for the salt-run courier. Northeast from Tortuga after neaps, edging for the Caicos water by the outer cays.
She carries modest sail; on starboard the top gallant shows a white patch. Captain eats in his cabin near dusk; takes a short noon sight.
In the cabin, third shelf down, a brown book; letters on the back: *H.J.K.* Do not open. Your first fair window is four days from now: the next in a fortnight."

Wrenn folded the paper and set it on the table.

"Four days," O'Connell said. "We spent one already so, we use today to prepare and tomorrow to gather men. We sail at dawn the day after."

"That's the line," Tyler said. They split the work.

"Wrenn," Tyler said, "we need a twin. Brown cover, plain spine, *H.J.K.* on the back if you can manage it. Find a binder who works fast."

"I know one," Wrenn said. "He binds ship journals and keeps his mouth shut."

"Jenkins," Tyler went on, "you'll handle the paper. Practice copying a figure clean, no flourishing. Same clerk's hand, tight and neat. We'll rehearse the swap until you can do it blind."

Jenkins nodded. "I'll need two hours and a quiet corner."

"O'Connell," Tyler said, "you get us a dock pass that will stand a hard stare and a small boat we can borrow without talk. Also, a cover story. We're not thieves… we're dull men with a tally error."

"Dull is my finest act," O'Connell said.

"Cobbs," Tyler said, "two smoke pots ready but capped. They're only to make eyes turn, not to scare men off their feet."

Cobbs scratched his beard. "Pitch, hemp, clay. I can set them by dusk."

Tyler looked at each man. "We keep to the rule. No killing unless we must save a life. We don't plunder. We take only what we came for." They broke.

The following morning…

Wrenn went out into the heat and found the binder in a lane off the fish market. The shop was three planks and a bench, but the man's hands were steady, and his awl was sharp.

He bought a plain brown notebook, a strip of thin leather, and a small box of brass letters. The binder pressed the letters into the back while the leather was warm, then trimmed the edges neat.

"You want a ribbon?" he asked.

"Red looks tidy." Wrenn nodded once and paid.

Back in the room, Jenkins worked at the table with a ledger he'd borrowed from the cooper, copying figures in a tight, small hand until they all looked like brothers.

He spoke the numbers under his breath as he wrote them. "Twelve… eight… two… carry one."

He swapped the real book for the blank one and back again without looking down. The first time he fumbled the ribbon.

The third time he didn't.

O'Connell walked the quay and came back with a dock chit that would pass immediately.

"Harbour boy who can't count," he said. "I fixed his mistake, and he called it a favor. We're now allowed to 'clarify a tally after hours.' You're welcome."

He also found a loaner skiff with muffled oarlocks and no owner who asked questions.

Cobbs cooked his smoke in a small clay pot over a slow flame. Pitch melted; hemp smoldered; clay warmed.

He capped it with a fitted lid and tied a long match to the handle. The second pot he packed the same way and wrapped both in canvas. "Only if we need a fuss," he said. "And never near dry rope."

They came back together near sunset and ran the rehearsal. Wrenn played the captain.

He stood by the shelf and reached for the third one down without looking.

Jenkins waited until the man's eyes were on the inkwell, then laid his blotting cloth, turned the ledger, and switched it for the twin with one hand. He closed the cover and set it back.

O'Connell counted out loud to make him hurry. "One... two... three... done." The fifth run was clean. The sixth was cleaner.

"Keep your face calm," Wrenn said. "Let your hands do the work."

They ate cold fish and drank water. Night came up slowly.

"Tomorrow," Tyler said, "we meet Pike at Dock C and finish the muster. We are buyers on board and nothing else. We sail at first light the next day."

"And the story?" O'Connell said.

"We're carrying a note from Customs about a missed line on last week's salt," Tyler said.

"We ask to copy one figure in the cabin book and leave. If we're pressed, we show Talbot's bond and ask them to bring their pen."

"And if they bar the door?" Cobbs asked.

"Then we back off and try again when the next window comes," Tyler said. "We don't break our own rule for speed."

The room grew quiet for a moment. The yard below ticked and creaked as the night breeze moved the wood.

Wrenn set the twin book on the table. The leather was plain, a little stiffer than the real thing would be.

On the back the pressed letters looked right in the lamplight: *H.J.K.*

He slid a strip of red ribbon between the pages and closed it.

"It will pass in a cabin at dusk," he said.

Jenkins held it and tested the weight. "Good enough," he said. "I'll switch and be gone before the man thinks to sneeze."

Tyler leaned on his hands.

"We keep it simple. We don't get clever at the rail, we don't argue. We don't run unless someone draws steel. If it smells wrong, we come away. We have another window in a fortnight."

O'Connell looked out the small window toward the black line of masts. "It won't smell wrong," he said. "It will smell like wet rope and a man who wants his supper. We'll be in and out."

"Then rest," Tyler said. "We're dull men tomorrow. The day after, we're ghosts."

They put the lamp out and lay down on their coats. Outside, a cart rattled past, and the fish market went quiet one stall at a time.

Somewhere, the church bell marked the hour. Before sleep took him, Tyler saw Sarah in the dark, wondering how she and the children were doing.

He closed his eyes and pictured the book: he pictured Jenkins' hands, O'Connell's voice at the rail, Cobbs' pot capped and harmless.

"There's no going back now," he said to the rafters, and let the room grow still.

They woke to gulls and the smell of hot pitch. From the room over the cooper's yard, they could see the brigantine lying easily in her berth, a patient shadow against the quay.

By midmorning Dock C had its usual noise: barrows rattling, men calling, water on planks.

Talbot arrived late enough to be noticed, early enough to be useful, Pike stood by the rail with his hat low and that look he wore when nothing would surprise him and very little would please him.

Wrenn had a list folded in his hand; the twenty-three marks from the other day. He didn't set a new board; he set his boot on a bollard and called names.

"Barlow."

The fair-headed Englishman from the dock house stepped forward with a sea chest and a wrapped bundle of tools. "Here."

"Mathurin Desroches."

"Ay." A Kreyol topman with tar on his cuffs and a steady eye.

"Pieter van Ryn."

The Dutch helmsman nodded once, silent as before. One by one they answered.

A quiet Spaniard: a woman in a sailor's coat who didn't bother with the boy voice this time and didn't need to; two islanders with arms like carpenters and legs like ropewalkers.

A lad O'Connell called "Sprat" because he had that look. Most had slept near the quay to be early.

Two names met silence.

"Woods." Nothing.

"Martin." A boy shook his head. "He ran last night," he said. "Took his coin and ran."

Tyler weighed the air a beat. "We plan for thin patches," he said to Pike.

"Have you got a man or two in your pocket?"

Pike's eyes ticked toward Talbot and back. "Maybe one."

Talbot didn't bother to turn his head. "I have got two," he said softly. "Waiting to be seen."

He flicked two fingers. One of his quiet men peeled away and returned half an hour later with a broad-shouldered Guadeloupean and a weathered Breton who smelled faintly of cod and old storms. Neither spoke much; both signed quickly.

"Twenty-three stands," Wrenn said.

"Good," Pike answered.

"Hands stow your gear under the forward grating. If your kit drips, the pump will get to know you."

There was a small laugh that made the deck feel more like work and less like worry.

Jenkins walked the line with a scrap of paper, confirming trades without making a fuss.

"Climb?" he'd ask, and a man would nod, and Jenkins would see in his hands whether the nod meant anything.

He put a quiet dot next to the helmsman; another next to Barlow; two next to Mathurin. He gave the woman a sideways glance.

"You keep time?"

She tapped the haft of her knife twice in perfect half-seconds and looked bored doing it. Jenkins smiled and put a dot there too.

A corporal from the *Compagnies Franches de la Marine* drifted over with two soldiers and a little boredom to spend. He looked at faces and gear as if shopping.

"*Vos permis*," he said.

Wrenn showed him the same chit as last time, Talbot's bond heavy in the wax.

"Charter for a month. Muster confirmed. No press on French subjects."

His French was tidy enough to pass and rough enough not to annoy. The corporal sniffed and muttered, "*C'est bon. Dépêchez-vous.*"

The corporal looked at the seal more than the words, the way men do. Talbot let a coin click against the plank with the casualness of a man setting down a glass.

Work began to bite. The bosun sent men where they'd be best and where they'd be least in the way: topmen to ratlines to prove they could still move in three directions at once; heavier backs to the casks; careful fingers to the blocks.

Pike had the pump handles tried, and the water casks knocked; he hated surprises that came from inside a hull.

O'Connell moved through the noise with a quarterdeck voice and a tavern ear. He found two men ready to fight about whose bundle had taken whose spot and ended it by swapping them both to the other side of the grating.

"There," he said. "Now you're both wrong and both right. Stow."

Cobbs kept quiet, as usual, but he checked his canvas parcel twice and made sure the smoke pots were where they would do the least harm and the most good: low, away from heat, a long match coiled loose and dry.

Wrenn took Jenkins aside in the shade of the mainmast and slid the twin book into his coat.

"Weight's right," he said. "Spine a little stiff, but at dusk no one marries a ledger."

"And the cover story?" Jenkins asked.

"Clean," Wrenn said. "Missed line on salt. Clerk can't sleep. Copy one figure and begone."

Tyler joined them, just in time to hear Jenkins say: "I can write the content in my sleep now," he said. "I won't. But I could."

"Good," Tyler said. He let a breath out and it didn't look like one.

They ate quick bread gone to leather at the edge, a slice of cold fish, water warm as breath. The sun climbed, then softened.

By mid-afternoon, a harbour boy wandered close and affected to kick at a coil of rope until Jenkins drifted his way.

The boy looked at the bond, nodded like a child who'd decided to be old for five minutes, and forgot to ask a second question. He wandered off whistling the wrong tune to a hymn.

By the last bell before evening, the rollcall was done. Twenty-three aboard.

The two backfills, learning where things were, Pike had his watch bill chalked in plain lines: even halves, no heroics, enough hands for pumps, enough for a boat.

"Hands sleep aboard," Pike said. "If you sing, do it quietly. We cast off first light tomorrow."

They stood a moment in the late light. The harbour shifted down a gear; voices thinned; the chapel bell tested its tongue once and then waited.

On the far street a barber's sign creaked and swung and was still.

"Final check," Tyler said.

Jenkins patted his coat where the pass lay folded. Wrenn touched the place where the twin ledger sat.

O'Connell nodded toward the loaner skiff they'd arranged to lift quietly. Cobbs tapped the canvas parcel with his boot.

"Good," Tyler said. "We move like men who've done this a hundred times and don't care to remember any of them."

They broke to their small jobs. Lines checked. Oars muffled. A word here, a nod there. Nothing loud, nor dramatic. The kind of day a harbour forgets before dark.

As the sun let go of the roofs and the first lamps took over, Tyler stood by the rail and looked once toward town. The barber's door was shut. The alley was empty. Good. He put his hand on the warm wood and felt the ship answer the touch—just a little.

"Dawn," he said.

"Dawn," O'Connell answered, and that was that.

They went below to borrow what sleep they could.

The brigantine settled. Dock C folded into its night shape. Far outside the mole the sea spoke in its slow, sure way, and somewhere under another sky a bigger ship turned her head the same way without knowing why.

Somewhere at sea – The Enforcer…

Night pressed low over the channel. The *Enforcer* moved with a long, patient roll, lanterns hooded, water whispering along her bow.

A blink of light off the starboard quarter: two short, one long —their own signal.

"Boat to leeward," Greaves said. "Dispatch."

"Luff and heave to," Davies ordered.

The small cutter slid in under their lee. A messenger came up the side with a canvas tube and a wet cap, breath steaming.

"Replies to your circular, sir."

Davies broke the wax, skimmed the top slips, then handed one to Greaves.

Reply No. 7 — per your notice:
Small boat, green strake, short mast — fits the Sea Fern.
Said to have been sold at Tortuga yesterday. She was seen leaving the mole before dusk, new men aboard, no name taken.
Word comes from the harbour watch, passed on by a paid runner.

Greaves looked up. "That puts them on Tortuga's tide."

Davies nodded once. "And on our chart."

He turned to the deck. "Mr. Simmons; bring her about. Set course for Tortuga. Keep her moving and keep her quiet."

"Aye, sir."

Canvas climbed; the frigate leaned into the new wind.

Davies kept the slip in his hand a moment longer, then tucked it into Tyler's log without opening the book.

"They're close," Greaves said.

"They'll stay that way," Davies answered.

The bell struck once, thin in the grey. The *Enforcer* swung onto the new course, sixty to eighty miles from Tortuga.

By late morning she would reach the island's line; toward the same dawn where Tyler's men slept on deck and their captain had said, 'Dawn.'

CHAPTER IX

Close Encounters

The brigantine slipped from the harbour in the pre-dawn chill. For Tyler, standing watch at the rail, the first hours were always the worst. Every sail was a potential threat, but today, they were hunting one in particular.

They cleared the headland before the sun had any heat. By late morning, the island was a low smear. By afternoon, nothing but water and sky.

Pike kept her steady, his good eye narrowed against the glare. "North-by-east," he said. "Don't look eager."

They didn't.

They worked the small work: lines coiled, blocks checked, a frayed lashing re-tarred. A crew pretending to be bored, their nonchalance a carefully maintained lie.

Jenkins ran the handwriting twice on a scrap and stopped. Wrenn kept the twin book inside his coat, his fingers brushing the spine in a nervous tic. Cobbs checked his canvas parcel once and then ignored it.

Toward the falling light, the sea grew that half-hour older a sailor can feel with his eyes closed. Pike stood with the glass and did not speak until he had to.

"There," he said, voice low. "A quarter point on the starboard bow. Small topsail. Patch like a cloud on the top gallant." He lowered the glass. "Talbot's courier."

Tyler took one look and nodded, the weight of command settling on his shoulders. "We do it as we said."

Pike eased canvas; the brigantine lost a little speed and drifted into the courier's wake like a man falling in step with another on a street. No rush. No crowding. Just close enough for a voice.

"Skiff," O'Connell said, already moving. They lowered the little boat without a slap.

O'Connell took the after oar, his big hands making the wood seem small. Jenkins climbed in with the pass folded neat and a blotter under his coat. Wrenn followed with the twin book and the look of a man who had explained small mistakes to strangers before.

"Don't shout," Pike called. "You're tired men with a dull problem."

They pulled for the courier. She was what Talbot had promised: a tidy little salt-run sloop with a patched topsail and a captain who liked his deck picked up.

Two hands watched them over a coil. The captain stood by the cabin door, small, careful, eyes that didn't waste much.

"Ho the boat," he said. Wrenn lifted the pass without flourish.

"Dock chit," he said. "Customs sent us out. Tally error on last week's salt. Clerk can't sleep. We'll copy one line and leave you to your supper."

The captain looked at the wax, not the words, and then at their faces. "I do not like my papers touched."

"I wouldn't either," Wrenn said. "We'll write on ours. Your hand stays yours."

A beat, a long blink, then the captain jerked his chin toward the little cabin.

"One man," he said. "No ink on my table."

"Two men," Wrenn said mildly. "One to write, one to keep his elbows. No ink on your table."

Another beat. "Two," the captain allowed.

He pointed at O'Connell. "Not that one. He looks like he likes his elbows."

O'Connell grinned and let the boat drift back a foot. "I'll keep the sea company."

Wrenn and Jenkins climbed aboard slow and tidy. No sudden moves, no talk they didn't need. The captain led them below into a cabin the size of a good cupboard. It smelled of salt, lemon oil, and a day's worth of air.

The captain planted himself with his back against the only door, not rude, just final. To his left was a shelf—third down—books tight as teeth.

"Quick," he said.

Wrenn stood where he could see the captain without looking at him. He set the blotter down like a man putting his hat aside.

"Here," he said softly, and his eyes told Jenkins which shelf.

Jenkins moved like he had done it a hundred times. Right hand to the third shelf; fingers on a brown back stamped *H.J.K.*

He eased the volume out, shifted another half a spine as though making room, and set it on the captain's blotter like a man clearing his table. In that same breath the twin was in its place.

Wrenn slid the real *H.J.K.* under his coat, tight against his ribs, before the decoy ever moved.

Jenkins opened the twin as if it had never been shut, turned a page, let his eyes linger. He made a mark on his scrap; the sort of figure any clerk might scratch to keep a captain satisfied. The ship creaked. Footsteps crossed overhead. The captain breathed.

"Done?" the captain asked.

"Done," Jenkins said.

He closed the twin, let the ribbon fall where it pleased, and slid it back onto the shelf without a glance.

He picked up the blotter and his scrap. Under its shadow, Wrenn buttoned the real *H.J.K.* against his coat: nothing to see, nothing to find.

Wrenn folded the pass back into his pocket without making a show of it. "Thank you for your time," Wrenn said. "Sleep now. The clerk will."

The captain watched them both a little bit longer than was comfortable, then stepped aside.

"Go," he said.

They came up and into the cooler air.

O'Connell had the skiff trimmed and ready. Wrenn went over the side first.

Jenkins followed with the same care he'd used handling the book. No one ran. No one pretended not to hurry. They just did what they had come to do and left.

"Trouble?" O'Connell asked under his breath.

"None," Wrenn said. "He hates clerks. That helped." They pulled back.

On the brigantine, Pike let her slide a little farther off as if making room for a friend. The courier kept her line and did not look back.

Tyler waited by the rail, the tension in his jaw finally easing. Jenkins handed up the scrap, the numbers written small and neat. Wrenn handed up the empty, calm look of a man who had expected argument and found none.

"Clean," Jenkins said.

Tyler nodded once. "Good. Let's not be clever now."

They hooked on the tackles and brought the skiff aboard the way they had lowered it. No slap, no scrape, not even a curse.

Cobbs put a tarp over the canvas parcel as if it were something that didn't matter at all.

O'Connell coiled the painter twice and hung it where a painter likes to hang.

Pike gave her a touch more canvas. The brigantine leaned, found her old gait, and the gap between the two ships began to grow like a stiff page turning.

"Course?" Pike asked.

"Hold it till full dark," Tyler said. "Then we slide off a point and let the night eat our wake."

"Aye."

They ate late: bread, a bite of meat, water with a taste of barrel. No one talked much. When they did, it was short.

"Ribbon?" O'Connell said.

"Sat where it wanted," Jenkins said. "Didn't fight me."

"Captain?" Cobbs asked.

"Small. Careful," Wrenn said. "Counted to three before he spoke."

Pike stood with the glass, watching nothing. "He'll forget us by morning," he said.

"Good," Tyler said. He put a hand to the rail and let the wood answer back. For a tick he saw Sarah in his mind, her smile a stark contrast to the grim work of the day and then put her where he kept her—safe and steady, not too near and not far.

The first stars came up, the wind held.

The ship settled into the dark the way a body settles into a bed it knows. Somewhere behind them, a small sloop's captain wrote one line in his own book and did not think of the men who had written a line in theirs.

"Steady," Pike said.

"Steady," Jenkins echoed.

They ran on, dull on purpose, and the sea made that small sound along the planks that tells a sailor he has done nothing wrong yet.

By late afternoon the next day, Tortuga rose out of the haze: low hills, white scabs of surf, the line of the mole like a finger pointing out to sea. The brigantine held its course, easy as a cart on a good road.

Tyler shaded his eyes, then lifted his hand. "Glass."

Pike passed it without looking away from the water. Tyler took a long, steady look. A familiar cut of hull sat beyond the mole, riding like a thought you couldn't shake.

Fine entry, proud bowsprit, three clean tiers of canvas waiting. He didn't need the figurehead to know her. A cold knot tightened his stomach.

"The *Enforcer*," he said, voice flat.

O'Connell was at his shoulder before he'd finished the word, his usual grin absent. "Here?"

"Here," Tyler said. He handed the glass to Pike.

"Quartermaster?"

"I'm thinking the same thing you are," O'Connell said. "Our faces don't touch that quay."

Pike lowered the glass. "Frigate is anchored off the main roadstead. French are letting them sit polite, which means they'll let them see everything. If we walk in by the mole, we'll be counted coming and going."

"We can't wait," Tyler said, the weight of their dwindling time pressing on him. "Talbot's book…"

Pike looked at the coast instead of their faces. "There's a way in that isn't a quay," he said.

"Saint-Nicolas' headland, lee side. Locals call it Goat's Cut. Shallow teeth, narrow throat. A brig would knock her bottom out. A yawl will slide through on the half-tide if your man can read colour in water."

"Boats then," Tyler said.

"Or you swim," Pike added, and made a face that said he already knew the answer to that.

Wrenn patted his coat again, a subconscious gesture of protection. "I'm not swimming a ledger flourish."

"Boats," Tyler confirmed. "We put two ashore quiet. One carries the book, the other keeps eyes."

O'Connell's jaw worked. "They will be launching cutters for a stroll every hour if they're smart. They'll sweep the mole, Customs, and the fish quay first. Those are the places we shouldn't be."

"Agreed," Tyler said. "We stay away from the mole, from Customs. We do not show ourselves at the fish quay." He glanced to Wrenn.

"Do you have a way to put the book in Talbot's hand that isn't a door in daylight?"

Wrenn thought a moment. "Not a door," he said.

"A bench. Back of *Rue du Sel*—salt street—behind the second warehouse with blue shutters. There's an old winch bedded in sand.

Two short chalk lines on the winch post were always his mark for 'drop under the eaves within five minutes. I've used it twice. Different years. Different reasons."

"Good," Tyler said. "You'll use it a third."

Jenkins, quiet until now, said, "If they're watching those places, they'll be watching chalk."

"Not if we don't lay it," Wrenn said.

"We'll bring the mark with us. Talbot has a woman sits there afternoons, green scarf. *Mireille*. She sells bait on days she doesn't sell news. I'll put the book in her hand. She'll walk it to him without leaving a shadow to follow."

Pike let the brigantine fall off a hair, putting the island on their beam and the sun at their backs.

"If you're taking Goat's Cut," he said, "you go in with the tide rising. Gives you more water under the keel and fewer surprises on the rocks. We'll hold off out here. The small boats can slip inside over the flats, but you'll have maybe an hour before the tide turns.

"Wrenn, Jenkins with the page," Tyler said. "O'Connell, you take the skiff and sit inside the shadows just outside the Cut.

If a French patrol wanders, you are fishermen who went too far for bait. Cobbs—keep your smoke where it is. No flair unless it saves a life."

Cobbs grunted. "Clay is capped. I'll keep it sulking."

Tyler held out a hand. Wrenn passed him the folded copy. Tyler didn't unfold it. He just looked at Wrenn. "Oilskin."

Wrenn slid a waxed oilskin-wrapped book sleeve sized for a small ledger from his coat, wrapped the *H.J.K.* volume inside, tied it with twine, and stowed the parcel flat under his shirt against his ribs.

"Do it now," Tyler said. "Do it slow."

They did it on the after rail, out of the wind. Jenkins checked the figures one last time, not because he doubted himself, but because he knew men doubted paper when it mattered. He also checked the binding and the tie, then pressed the wax seam along the fold so the parcel lay flat and dry.

Pike watched the frigate with the glass, measured and unworried. "They're lying easy," he said.

"Two boats down. One towing for show. They'll parade the pennant and look useful. They won't see a yawl that hugs rock like a lover."

"Let's not give them a romance," O'Connell said, already at the davits.

Tyler looked at the island again. The water over the flats showed shades—teal, then pale, then white where coral shouldered up. He put his hand to the rail, the way he always did before sending good men into tight water.

"Signals," he said. "If Goat's Cut looks false—"

"We turn," Wrenn said. "No cleverness on a falling tide."

"Good," Tyler said. "And if you can't make it to *Mireille*, you use the winch. Two lines. Then you walk away like you forgot why you came."

"Understood," Wrenn said.

They brought the yawl inboard, oars muffled, tiller wrapped. O'Connell dropped into the skiff and tested her roll with his knees.

Jenkins climbed to the yawl's thwart, light as a cat. Wrenn went last, one hand to the gunwale, one to his chest where the oilskin rode.

Pike eased the brigantine to a long, gentle hove-to. Canvas

slatted once, settled. The ship took the swell with a patient shoulder.

"Half-flood," he said. "Go."

They lowered away and took the first bite of water with soft oars. The brigantine fell behind them in three breaths. Ahead, the island widened and flattened, and the sound changed. Reef noise is its own thing—low and constant, like someone talking in the next room.

O'Connell steered for the deeper colour, eyes on the little ripples that meant teeth. Twice he checked, once with the blade, once with the pole.

"Left," he said quietly, and the yawl slid a yard and dodged something sharp enough to teach a man a lesson he'd remember for a month.

"Pretty," Jenkins breathed.

"Ugly," O'Connell said. "That's why it works."

They found the throat—two dark shoulders of rock with a ribbon of green between. The swell leaned in and then forgot about them.

Inside, water turned slick and shallow and warm; mangrove roots wrote their names in the tide.

"Here," Wrenn said, pointing to a strip of sand no wider than a longboat. No smoke. No houses. Just a path chewed by bare feet and goats.

"Skiff sits," O'Connell said. "I'll keep her moving like a man afraid of mosquitoes."

Wrenn and Jenkins stepped out into calf-deep water, lifted the yawl just enough to miss a stone, and ran her onto sand without a scrape. Jenkins wiped his hands, more out of habit than need.

"Back in an hour," Wrenn told O'Connell. "If we're not here, we're fine. If we're here and moving too fast, you're fishing men again."

O'Connell nodded once.

Wrenn and Jenkins took the goat path into the brush. The air smelled of wet leaves, salt, and the faint sour of yesterday's rum.

They moved at a pace that looked like a walk and felt like a run. Twice they froze and let a patrol of French soldiers pass on a higher track; bull's-eyes hooded even in daylight, muskets balanced by men who wanted the day to end.

They came out behind *Rue du Sel* where the warehouses leaned toward each other and made their own weather.

A woman with a green scarf sat on a bench, mending a net. She didn't look up when Wrenn sat at the far end. He set his palm on the plank between them, lifted it, and left nothing a man could swear to in a court.

Jenkins sneezed once, too loud, which was the old signal Wrenn and Talbot had used when chalk was too dear.

Mireille tied off her thread, gathered her net, and rose. She didn't touch the place on the bench. She drifted toward a door painted the colour of old sky, slipped inside, and let the door close after her heel.

Wrenn didn't move for a slow count of forty. Jenkins watched the alley that wasn't there until you needed it.

When the count ended, Wrenn stood. "Back door," he said.

They took a different path to the trees and came down to the sand in the shade of a mangrove. The skiff was there, gnats dancing over O'Connell's hat brim. He didn't ask and they didn't tell.

"Good?" O'Connell said.

"Enough," Wrenn answered.

They pushed off. Behind them the island kept its secrets. Ahead, over the reef's low talk, the brigantine lay where they had left her, a patient, dark shoulder against the swell. Farther out, a frigate's topmasts made a comb against the sky: quiet for now, but not blind.

"Row," O'Connell said, light and steady.

Night pressed in. Tortuga's harbour showed a few soft lights; farther out a warship sat like a dark thought that wouldn't leave.

Pike had the glass, then handed it back as if it burned. "I'm not taking this ship anywhere near that pier while an English frigate watches," he said. "I don't work for the gallows."

"We've paid Talbot," Tyler said, frustration edging his voice.

"Jack said his Quartermaster would find us once the debt was settled. I need that meeting."

"You need air in your lungs more," Pike snapped. "Stay under those guns and you'll lose both."

O'Connell drifted up from the shadows. "He's right about one thing; we show our faces in that harbour; they'll count us by lantern light. Names and boots."

Wrenn folded his arms. "Word will travel without us standing on the quay. Talbot has the book."

Tyler shook his head. "Every hour we hide, the bond runs down.

We still don't have a ship of our own. We don't have a crew that answers to us... only hires. And Jack is the key to both. Waiting kills time we don't have."

Pike's voice went flat. "And walking into Tortuga kills you. Pick which funeral you want."

Silence held long enough to feel the ship breathing.

"Compromise," O'Connell said.

"We don't sit under the frigate. We don't dock. We slide behind the headland and disappear. One night only. If Jack's man shows, good. If not, we leave before dawn and stop giving the Navy easy guesses."

Pike looked at Tyler, then over Tyler's shoulder at the quiet black shape beyond the mole.

"One night," he said. "No lamps. No songs. No stamping on the deck like cows. Anyone coughs, cough into your sleeve."

Tyler stared at the harbour until the lights blurred. He hated the feel of time slipping, of Sarah waiting for a future he couldn't yet secure. "One night," he agreed. "Then we're gone."

Pike gave a short nod and turned to the wheel. "We'll tuck into a small cove behind the headland. Close water, high rock. If a cutter comes nosing in, we're already moving out. No one stands on the rail. No one leans over to stare at his own doom."

"Wrenn," Tyler said, "if a message comes, it'll come. We don't help it by being obvious."

"It'll come if it's meant to," Wrenn answered. "And if not, we'll still be breathing."

Cobbs came up with his canvas bundle and set it down like a sleeping dog. "You want smoke if they sniff us?"

"No," Pike said. "If they sniff us, we're already late. Keep that for when the sea is the only judge."

They eased off the coast and slipped along the dark shoulder of land. The wind softened under the cliff. Water changed its sound.

Pike steered them into a pocket of black where the island held its breath. They let the ship drift, then set a small hook and a line ashore. Nothing clanked. Nothing flashed.

"Set watches," Pike said, low. "Four men at a time. Whisper if you must talk. If you have a song in you, keep it for another life."

Men settled like shadows. The hull rocked slowly and patiently.

Tyler stayed by the rail. O'Connell stood with him, saying nothing. Wrenn leaned nearby, eyes half-closed, reading the night like a book he'd already learned by heart.

Jenkins checked the folded permits in his coat for the tenth time and put them back. Cobbs sat on his heels with his back to the mast and looked like he could sleep through a war and wake to fire it.

"Until dawn," Tyler said. "If no one comes, we slip out and keep moving."

"And stop counting days out loud," Pike added. "It makes them run faster."

Tyler almost smiled and didn't. He tried not to think of Davies, because thinking of Davies never helped.

The cove held them like a closed hand. Far away, the frigate fired a single salute to its own importance, and the sound arrived thin and late. The crew breathed. The ship breathed. Time walked.

One night. Then the sea.

CHAPTER X

Sarah's Resolve

The bell did not ring at sunset. No crier, no notice nailed to a post. One evening the sound simply failed to come, and the lane outside remembered how to breathe in its old way.

Wheels squeaked; the mule that dragged the baker's cart decided to stop and be persuaded; a door banged and stayed open. The Watch passed two at a time instead of four, boots tired rather than angry. Relief, when it comes, is quieter than fury.

Sarah stood half a step back from the curtain so her shadow would not print on the cloth. The fabric was thin and clean because Ruth Calder, her cousin, kept it that way: boil, scrub, rinse, wring, hang—order as religion. Fear obeyed Ruth less than flour did, but fear obeyed her more than it obeyed most people.

"Eat," Ruth said without turning from the small hearth. "Before your hands shake and you pretend they don't."

"I will," Sarah said. "After I write." Keep the voice steady. Children hear the tremble first.

Tom sat at the table with a slate and a thumb-smudged stub of chalk, chewing a number the way a boy chews a crust. Lizzie knelt on the boards with a wooden horse whose head had been glued twice and dared the seam to fail a third time.

The room smelled of soap, boiled onion, old wood, warm wet linen, and a thread of smoke from the brazier, domestic courage.

Sarah laid paper flat and set the ink where a careless sleeve could not kiss it. First lines must be plain. Plain travels farther.

To the Secretary of the Admiralty, London.

Sir,
I write as the wife of William Tyler, late Captain of His Majesty's frigate Enforcer.
I request an inquiry, not favor.

A proclamation in Port Royal names my husband a traitor. He refused to be used as a screen for unlawful traffic conducted by the Governor, Sir Thomas Sevington, and his agent, Mr. Edward Norton. For this he is hunted.
He was shown a denial of promotion whose timing cannot be correct. I ask that the registers in London and Jamaica be compared.

I remain,
Sarah Tyler

She sanded the ink, blew once, folded twice and twice again, tied it with kitchen string. The wrapper bore a name Wrenn had said in an even voice: a clerk who opened the right drawer and did not talk at supper. Ruth watched the neat hands and nodded once, approval disguised as economy.

"Tom," Sarah said.

He came as if he'd been waiting. "Yes, Mother."

"If someone knocks and the knock is wrong, you fetch Ruth. If a man in the lane asks a question, you ask his name first. Two questions before one answer. If your belly turns cold, you come by the back steps and count to twenty before you speak."

Tom nodded, jaw brave in the way boys think brave looks. She smoothed his hair. It smelled of sweat and chalk and worry.

Lizzie looked up, solemn. "Does the horse have a name?"

"Today," Sarah said, "his name is Patience."

"Give him a brother and call him Quiet," Ruth said, and the corner of her mouth moved, which was Ruth's smile.

The knock came: two soft taps, one back—the agreed pattern. Ruth lifted the latch only after checking the floor dust lay exactly as she had left it. It did.

Wrenn's man stepped in sideways, cap low, shoes scuffed, mouth careful. A face the world forgets after looking once, an earned skill.

"Good morning," he said, which meant no eyes behind me. Sarah gave him the letter. He did not weigh it like bad men do; he made it part of himself in one small motion—inside the coat, under the ribs—where knives hide better but a letter must learn to as well.

"A horse to Kingston," he said. "A packet after that. I'll choose the second, not the first."

"Good," Sarah said. "Leave me no marks."

"No marks," he repeated, then let his eyes find Tom and Lizzie and move on. Looking at children makes a man human; human is how men die in lanes. He left as he came.

Ruth let the latch settle. Sarah put her palm flat on the table; wood is honest if you let it be.

Ruth set a plate. "Eat," she said again, softer. Sarah ate.

The onion was mean to the eyes, and she let it. Tears with a reason are easier than the other kind.

The lane outside practiced ordinary: a woman laughed and remembered not to; a boy ran without looking like he was fleeing; a hawker sang the wrong notes and didn't care. The Watch passed without counting windows.

The house held still and learned the new silence.

When Tom's hand cramped around the chalk, Sarah warmed his fingers around a cup.

"The letters between numbers," she said, "matter as much as the numbers." Tom nodded like he would try to believe her.

She wrote an address on a second wrapper and tucked it in Ruth's thread box. Ruth's eyes approved.

"We keep nothing," Ruth said, as if reminding a child to put his shoes side by side.

"Nothing," Sarah said. "Except what we can carry in here." She tapped her temple and did not look at the door.

When night came, Tom curled around his slate, Lizzie slept with the wooden horse clutched like a kitten, and Ruth's needle ticked its little clock. Sarah lay awake and counted to twenty, then fifty, then stopped counting. Numbers imply ownership. Nobody owns the dark.

In the deep of it, Ruth's voice: "Write." Not a command; permission. Sarah trimmed the candle, set it where light would not print on the curtain, warmed her fingers over the brazier's last ember, and took up the pen again.

Morning made a pale square on the wall and then a brighter one. Somewhere a cart lost a wheel and swore about it; somewhere a hen advertised an egg as if it were a crown. Curfew was gone; caution remained.

The day moved forward the way you carry a chest with two people: a hand on each end, breathing together.

"We send two things today," Ruth said, laying mending on the table.

"One for men who love stamps. One for men who love ledgers."

Sarah nodded.

"Words small," she said. Her hand knew the size of what would pass where it needed to go.

The second letter was less plea than record—a thing a clerk might tuck where rain could not find it and pull out later when men argued about dates.

> Sir,
>
> I beg leave to lay a plain account. My husband, Captain William Tyler, returned to Port Royal three days before the great storm.
>
> He was sent for by His Excellency the Governor. The next morning a proclamation was cried in the town that my husband had refused a direct order from the Crown.
>
> Before any appeal could be made, watchers came to our door and officers of the Governor questioned members of my husband's crew. A night curfew was laid at once.
>
> My husband has served fifteen years without blemish. He has never, in my knowledge, disobeyed a lawful command. He spoke of papers shown him that bore a Royal seal; yet what followed was so sudden that I fear the seal did not carry the Royal will.
>
> I humbly ask that no sentence be passed upon hearsay from Port Royal until a neutral officer examines the Governor's letters against the Admiralty dispatches and harbour logs; that the dates of any London orders be compared with packet arrivals; and that statements be taken from the Harbour Office concerning

permits issued in those days.

I do not send this through the Governor's hands. I entrust it to a captain bound for England who does not know my name. If there is fault in me for writing, I accept it; but I beg an inquiry for my husband, whose whole service belongs to His Majesty.

I remain, Sir, your obedient servant,
Sarah Tyler

She dried the ink with sand, folded the sheet tight, and sealed it with plain wax.

"Where will it live?" Ruth asked, meaning How will it leave.

"In a seam," Sarah said.

She took a pillowcase from the mending pile, flattened the hem, slid the letter into the inside lip, and put three tack stitches through paper and cloth: small, tidy, the kind your hands make without looking.

If a man tugged, he'd lift scraps. If the right hands found the seam, it would become paper again.

Tom watched, eyes wide. "Is that magic?"

"It's a chore," Ruth said.

"Chores are the only magic that works every time."

They burned drafts in the brazier: the practice hands, the crossed-out starts. Ash turned slow as dull snow. Lizzie reached; Sarah caught her wrist gently.

"Not this," she said. "This mess is ours."

The knock came, the right rhythm, but softer. A different boy this time, thin as a rail, moving backward through the door as if the lane itself had pushed him in.

He lifted the laundry basket without looking inside, the way boys do when they are trying not to be curious.

Ruth scolded him for being late; he grinned and said he was early; Ruth told him twice as much then. It was a play with three lines, and everyone knew their cue.

He left in the same quiet way. He would walk to the yard that always came to the houses.

Wrenn's careful-mouthed man, or another like him, would meet the basket in a place the town had stopped seeing. The pillowcase would become a letter at a table where nobody counted socks out loud.

When the wrong knock came in the afternoon—heavy, impatient—Ruth opened, because doors you do not open get kicked.

"Search," the first man said, pushing like he wanted to be remembered by the wood. Ruth sidestepped and made him trip his pride on her silence.

They did the stupid dance. Lifted the mattress: straw. Opened the chest: shirts. Tapped the wall: wood.

A man looked too long at Tom and then away because he saw himself a dozen years ago and hated it.

Lizzie fed the wooden horse an imaginary carrot and did not cry. The men left with nothing to say, and the latch came back to Ruth's palm like a dog that knows its name, tea after.

Water is an answer to many things that are not questions. Ruth set cups, and the chine clinked just once.

Tom hovered by the table. "Will Father read our letters?" he asked.

"Not first," Sarah said. "First the men who decide what letters mean. Then, if the world remembers how to be fair, your father."

"Do they decide right?" he said.

"Not always," Sarah said. "But paper makes it harder to lie." She said it to him and to herself.

They made a small list: locket, papers, bread, water, shawl, slate, horse. Writing the list loosened something behind Sarah's ribs. Paper tames fear just enough to let a day happen.

Sarah ran stitches through a seam she had already mended. Doing a thing you can control lends you height against the things you cannot. Ruth's needle ticked.

Lizzie fell asleep mid-story, horse under chin. Tom practiced an R. Ruth would not praise until it deserved it.

When sleep came, Sarah took it in coins. Little ones, but they paid something.

The night hung like cloth, heavy and not in a hurry. The lane breathed its great animal breath. A coal winked in the brazier. Tom's quiet snore answered Lizzie's sigh. Ruth mended in the chair until the thread itself looked sleepy.

"Write," Ruth said again, and Sarah did.

Sir,

This is to set a record. After my husband was called to the Governor's house, a proclamation was cried that he had refused orders. That day and the next, men watched our door and questioned sailors' wives and messengers. A curfew was laid at once. We were warned that arrest would follow.

I ask only those dates be compared: any letter naming my husband a traitor, with packet departures recorded at the Harbour Office and Registry; and the Governor's orders, with any Admiralty dispatch that could have arrived in that time. If the times do not fit, I beg inquiry before judgment is passed. I do not send this through Port Royal. It would be read by the men it names.

Your obedient servant,
Sarah Tyler

She pricked the folded square into the hem of a tea cloth, three small stitches; the way you tack a thought inside your own head so even you cannot argue it away. She ran a thumb along the seam and felt the paper there like a small hard truth.

The knock, right again, gentler for the hour. Wrenn's careful-mouthed man slid in. Thinner in the face. Road dust on his cuffs.

"First letter is on the packet," he said. "Not the first packet. The second. I watched her take water."

Something small and stubborn in Sarah lifted like a bird.

"This one," she said, and Ruth handed him the cloth. He draped it over his arm like laundry, which it was, and like a letter, which it also was.

"I'll take the long road," he said.

"Spanish Town first, then Kingston. Too many eyes on the straight way."

He touched his hat a finger's width to the children and left backward so the lane would not feel watched.

Ruth's eyes followed him to the latch, measured the night, and measured Sarah. "Eat," she said, because the body must be bribed to keep faith.

Afterwards, the long part—the counting without wanting to, the doors your mind tries for the thousandth time.

Sarah refused the wrong pictures: refused William shot in a lane, refused William drowned in a culvert. She gave the dark nothing it could keep.

Toward morning, Tom lifted his slate. "Can I write a line?" he whispered.

"Choose one." He chose a line about truth. Wrote it once, careful; again, smaller; a third time, nearly even. "Does writing make it true?" he asked.

"It makes it harder to pretend it isn't," she said, brushing his hair back and leaving her hand there for one breath because he was too sleepy to mind.

Dawn built itself out of grey and then out of colour. The lane began its song: bucket, wheel, oath, hen, the hawker's wrong tune again.

Ruth teased a live ember out of ash and made tea out of the memory of heat.

"If the wrong knock comes today," Ruth said, "I open. You take the children to the corner and look at the floor. We don't rehearse arguments with men who like to win them."

"Yes," Sarah said. She set the locket in the flour jar, cold metal telling the truth about heat, then took it back out again because she didn't trust flour not to be stolen.

They folded two more blank wrappers; ready is a form of prayer. They waited, and waiting is work. They did it well.

By noon, a woman on the lane shouted at a dog that had eaten a loaf, then laughed and shoved the dog away with her knee. A man sang a hymn like a tavern song, and nobody corrected him. The world, practiced, began to sound accidentally normal.

Sarah notched thread, mended a sleeve, and thought of London—desks, lamps, men who liked pens and rules and the way their coats shone. She wrote for the man who cared about lists more than people.

The right words must find that hand first. Paper moves slowly; truth slower; she would make them walk the same road.

Late afternoon brought the third right knock of the day—soft, the rhythm changed by caution. A different runner stood there, older, the kind of man with a back that had learned to be invisible without bending.

He did not step inside; Ruth did not invite him. She held the laundry basket in the doorway, soap strong enough to hide a letter's breath, and he took it with the bored grace of someone who had carried heavier things for worse men.

"Watch the ditch at the Spanish Town road," Ruth said like she was talking about weather.

"It has a puddle that never dries," he said back, which meant I know. He went. The children exhaled. The room let out a long breath too.

Evening slid in. The horse on the table got a crumb. Tom named the horse's brother Quiet. Ruth didn't laugh; she gave the horse a job, guard the cloth, and the horse did it as hard as wood can.

In the meantime – Under the Governor's Residence…

Norton preferred a room that could be washed. The one he used for ugly work had lime on the walls and a floor that took water like a dock. The lamp hissed.

The air smelled of oil, dust, and lime. Ogdenville stood with his hands in his sleeves, the way men do who like their wrists unremarkable.

"Begin," Norton said, as if starting accounts, not ending lives.

On paper there were errands, movements, notes that meant

nothing when read alone: deliver, collect, confirm.

In his head he gave it a name, *Purification*, and the word pleased him enough that he did not smile. Smiling wastes information.

They did not strike like storms; storms are remembered. They moved like low water under pilings: silent, patient, gone before you look.

A lamp-maker who had once opened a wall for Wrenn stood in his own doorway, surprised that his hand miscounted coin on a night it never miscounted before.

The woman who sold string and news and laughter was asked to unlock a cupboard she had opened a hundred times; she did not open another.

A boy with proud feet was lifted by the collar just long enough to make him slow; he sat down somewhere no one would trip.

No crowd gathered. Crowds give days names and Norton hated named days.

He kept score by absence.

The next evening, lamps did not bloom in a certain corner. A stall with thread had nothing to sell but thread. A runner who normally crossed St. Matthew's twice by noon did not cast his shadow there once.

The town's web slumped, strands cut where fingers had learned to read.

Wrenn's careful-mouthed courier, who had watched the second packet take water, took the long road, as he had said, and was followed out of Spanish Town by men who knew roads better than towns.

Not close enough to make him run. Not far enough to lose

him in a crowd that did not exist on that strip of track.

They shadowed him past cane, past scrub where low trees keep secrets, into a notch between two hills where sound sits down and rests.

Ogdenville stepped out because he likes to ask his own questions.

"Where do you carry?" he asked. A professional question, like asking a wheelwright how he keeps the rim tight.

"Where I'm sent," the courier said. Truth. Lies wouldn't save him; truth wouldn't either.

"Names," Ogdenville said. The careful mouth did what it had been trained to do—gave up a dead man and a man already gone. Ogdenville's eyelids moved, his version of displeasure, then nodded. The courier answered nothing else anywhere, ever.

Norton did not write this down. He didn't need to.

Memory serves men like him when paper should not. He traced Wrenn's chalk marks in his head—two short lines on a post meaning under the eaves in five minutes; a boy whistling the wrong hymn on purpose to say no eyes; a laundry basket heavier than it looked.

You cannot pluck a web to pieces without making the spider feel; he cut enough strands to make the web sag.

"Leave the boy alive," Norton said aloud. Ogdenville inclined his head. Rooke would live and call it luck. Luck with a leash.

That night a watcher stood under Ruth Calder's eaves: the sort of man who can stand for an hour and look like he isn't. Soap, onion, children. Slate taps. A needle ticking its neat clock.

A woman's voice saying a child's name the way you say a prayer when you do not trust heaven.

The watcher did nothing, because nothing was the order. He

left at the number he'd been given. Houses that have nothing but stubbornness bite back on different nights.

Sarah noticed absences she did not speak aloud. The lamp on the corner never lit. The thread-woman's laugh went missing and did not come home. Footsteps that usually passed at a certain hour skipped the lane twice and then again.

She did not say Wrenn's name because names are tinder. Ruth did not say it either. They moved quietly around the emptiness like people do when someone is sleeping in a room you can't see.

Sarah set the third wrapper in the thread box and then took it out and put it in a crock and then put it back in the box. Tom watched the ritual without comment because children know when the rules of a room are not really about the room.

"Another letter?" He asked finally.

"In time," Sarah said. "We let the first ones walk ahead."

"Do letters get tired?" Lizzie asked, serious as a judge.

"They do," Ruth said. "But not as quick as men."

Norton burned a scrap of names in a dish and poured water on the ash. He didn't look at his reflection in the bowl. He dislikes being seen even by glass.

Ogdenville said, "Port Royal is quieter," without pride, because pride wastes ink.

"Clean enough," Norton said. He thought of London, a room he had never seen where men liked their pens and their rules, and the way light made their coats bright.

A letter waited there that told a story he had written with careful dates. He believed, as men like him do, that the first story to arrive becomes the ruler against which truth is measured.

He did not know about the square of paper already beyond his reach, stitched inside a tea cloth and carried the long road by a man who had learned to be invisible without dying of it.

Outside, Port Royal pretended ordinary. Inside houses like Ruth's, people did ordinary with the discipline of prayer. Ruth scrubbed.

Tom practiced a clean G. Lizzie told the wooden horse a secret and then told it again. Sarah set the locket in the flour and then took it out once more because the heart does not believe flour can keep anything safe.

They slept in pieces and woke in halves. Morning arrived, and they stood up in it. Waiting is work.

They did it, quiet and exact. The web held. Thin, broken in places, but it held… for now, for everyone: the ones who hunted, the ones who hid, and the ones who carried truth like a hot coal in a cup, looking for dry wood.

CHAPTER XI

Different Shores

Morning pressed a flat light over the water. The brigantine lay off the lee of the island, just far enough to feel the swell, just close enough to smell mangrove.

Out beyond the mole, three clean bands of sail and a proud bowsprit drew a neat comb against the sky.

You don't need a figurehead to know a ship you've led and loved. Tyler didn't say the name again. He didn't have to.

O'Connell stood near his shoulder the way men stand when they already know the answer.

Pike had the glass to his eye and that set look he wore when he'd decided not to be surprised by anything. He lowered the tube and rested both hands on the rail.

"She is still holding the main roadstead," he said.

"The French are letting them look polite, they are not rushing to leave until they found what they are looking for."

Tyler watched the tide line wrinkle and smooth. Time moved across the deck like a second wind. "We can't wait any longer," he said. "The longer we sit, the more eyes remember us."

"Then we don't wait," Pike said. His voice stayed level. "But we don't run into the lion's mouth either."

"Speak plain," Tyler said.

"Nassau," Pike answered. "We anchor on the wrong side, let

a curtain of bad manners hang between us and any English frigate. One frigate won't nose there alone for sport."

O'Connell made a face that wasn't quite a smile. "Hide in a den of thieves to dodge thieves in uniforms."

"It's a den with rules," Pike said. "Bad ones. But rules. You won't like them. They won't like you. That's what makes it work."

"Nassau wastes time," Tyler said.

"It buys some," Pike said.

"You want to hunt fog and a ship that went wrong? Do it with a dozen loud men around you who don't care what your face looks like. Do it where the Navy prefers not to look."

Jenkins came up quiet, hands behind his back like a clerk thinking of the next line.

"If we cut now, we make it in two nights. Breeze is clean. We use the time to ask soft questions about the *Valiant*, then turn back to meet Jack's man. Better than being counted by noon and chased by evening."

Cobbs scratched his beard. "Nassau's a nest. Put a foot wrong, something bites and won't spit you out."

"Don't put a foot wrong," Pike said.

"Don't swagger. Don't brag. Do your work then leave."

"Jack said his man would find us once Talbot was square," Tyler said.

"If he wants to, he will. Men like that always do." Pike answered.

Tyler let the quiet sit. The long part of the argument was over; the short part mattered most.

"If we go to Nassau," he said, "we go to listen, not to fight. Plain canvas and plain faces. Ask after a fog bank where none should be, and a British hull too big for her water. We come back with ears full or with trouble. You're telling me the first is likelier."

"I'm telling you it keeps you alive long enough to try," Pike said.

O'Connell folded his arms, thought, then gave one short nod. "I won't love it. But I see it."

Jenkins blew out through his nose. "I can live with pirates looking through me. I can't live with a broadside from a ship that knows my name."

Cobbs tapped the rail once with his knuckles. "If Nassau is where we sleep, we sleep light. If anyone asks for smoke, I say no until you say yes."

Tyler turned last to Wrenn. Wrenn stood with his coat buttoned, eyes on the far water, not the near talk.

"Well?" Tyler asked.

"Nassau holds you if you hold yourself," Wrenn said.

"Its law is money. Sometimes pride. Try not to wake the second."

Tyler nodded. He thought of Sarah's face by firelight, the children's voices in a small room, the weight of the locket in his pocket.

Every choice stole time from somewhere. He had to choose which pocket to empty.

"Set for Nassau," he said at last. "We go tonight."

Pike didn't smile; he never did. He turned his head and told the bosun: "Stand by." The word moved down the deck in a way the crew understood.

Tyler stayed with the rail a moment longer and looked at the frigate where his life had been. He let the feeling sit, then fold away. He'd take it out later when it was safer to hold.

"We go where we can breathe," he said, mostly to himself.

"And we don't make a poem about it," O'Connell said, because he couldn't help himself.

They went below to plan the rest like men who know plans are most useful before the first bell and after the last; and dangerous at any hour in between.

Pike's cabin was not grand. It was honest. A table with a lip so charts didn't wander. A bench that remembered other backs. A locker with a habit of closing the first time you asked it to. Tyler liked rooms like that. They made men talk sense.

O'Connell, Jenkins, Cobbs, and Wrenn took the bench. Pike stood, because standing was his way of telling a room he meant to keep moving.

The ship creaked around them like a big animal settling its shoulders.

Outside, men coiled and stowed; inside, paper waited.

Tyler laid the small chart flat. He didn't draw long lines. He put a finger on Tortuga, another on the Bahama tongue of water.

"We keep the island on our quarter until dusk," he said.

"Then we slide east enough to look like we're going somewhere respectable. Come dark, we lay off to the northwest and keep our wake small. Nassau by tomorrow night if the breeze stays friendly."

Pike grunted approval. "We don't moor in the harbour proper. We come down on the Hog Island side and anchor where sand holds and men in uniforms don't care to walk. We'll look like a coaster. We'll be one."

"What name?" Jenkins asked.

Pike slid a hand into his coat and brought out his daybook.

He had a page that didn't look like much and meant a great deal. "*Mercy Anne,*" he said.

"Owned by a man who can sign it and not be surprised. She carries salt and sometimes timber and never remembers too much."

Jenkins nodded and wrote the name on a scrap. O'Connell tapped the table with a finger.

"Nassau is loud because men want to be seen," he said. "We do the opposite. Two ashore at a time. No one sits in a tavern long enough to learn the songs. And we don't ask for the *Valiant* like we're buying a pie."

"How do we ask?" Cobbs said, not to argue, but to hear the shape of the thing.

"Like it's routine," O'Connell said.

"We ask after fog where no fog belongs. A British ship that came out of nowhere and didn't look right. Sailors who swore they saw a hull too big for the water under it. We don't put all of it in one mouth."

"Men who saw a fog that didn't belong will talk about it for free," Wrenn said.

"They like to bring their hands up and show you the size of it. Let them." He rubbed his left shoulder without thinking.

"There was a bank last season that made two boats argue with each other and not know it. Ask that way."

Tyler marked nothing on the chart. He didn't want to leave ink where another man's eye might rest later.

"Rules," he said, and O'Connell rolled his eyes in a friendly way that said here we go.

"No boasting," Tyler said. "No knives on tables. No jackets off where men might read arms and scars and make up stories. If someone bumps you, you move. If someone doubts your name, let him…

We don't bring a quarrel back to the boat. If a man starts to sing your past, you let him finish, you drink his drink, and you leave."

Pike scratched his jaw. "I won't be your priest," he said.

"If Nassau turns into a sermon I didn't ask for, I'll lift anchor and go find wind."

"Understood," Tyler said. "We're buying days, not trouble. We won't pay double."

Jenkins laid out a simple list and read it: "Pairs ashore at bell one and bell three. Questions asked twice, answered once. No one visits the same bench two days running. If anyone asks whose boat we are—"

"*Mercy Anne*," Pike said.

"—and if anyone asks where we carry next," Jenkins went on, "we shrug and let him tell us."

O'Connell rubbed thumb against forefinger, thinking. "We want fishermen, not captains. Captains lie for glory while fishermen lie only about the price of a net and the size of a catch."

Cobbs spoke last. "What about Jack?"

Tyler looked at Wrenn.

Wrenn lifted a shoulder and let it fall. "He said his Quartermaster would find us when the debt is paid. If he wants you, he'll have a way that doesn't make a fuss."

"Then we make ourselves easy to find without being stupid about it," Tyler said.

"Same hour, same small square, two mornings, then change. No chalk, no old signs. Feet and ears only."

Pike closed his daybook and set it aside. "If a Navy sail shows on the horizon while we're there, we go to ground behind Hog Island and look like a mistake. If a boat rows out from that pretty frigate out there, we look smaller than we are."

"And if someone decides we're interesting?" O'Connell asked.

"Then we're gone before he finishes deciding," Pike said.

They went round the table once more, not to add new ideas, but to pull out the ones that smelled like pride. Pride is noise and noise gets you caught.

"Two nights there," Tyler said.

"We listen. We leave. We keep the Passage in our heads like a tune you hum to yourself."

Wrenn looked at the door, the deck, his hands.

"There's something I need to say before we set it in motion," he said, but he didn't say it yet. He felt for the place the words ought to sit.

"Say it after we lift," Tyler said gently. "Say it where we can hear the water too."

Wrenn nodded once. He looked tired in the way men look when they've decided something that will change their shape.

Pike thumped the table with the heel of his hand. Not loud.

"We cast off at dusk," he said. "Eat. Sleep. Stow your pride."

They filed out to do the parts of a plan that never make a story—the cleanup, the tying down, the simple work of waiting without fidgeting until it's time to go.

The sun fell behind the island in a straight line and then in a hurry, as if someone had tugged the light by a string. The brigantine came round easily and let herself ride. On the shadowed side of the headland the water took the colour of old coin.

Wrenn stood by the quarter rail with his coat buttoned and his hat down. He rubbed his leg like a man who felt the weather more than other men did. Tyler joined him and waited until the quiet made words feel like the right size.

"You had a sentence earlier," Tyler said, not making it a question.

Wrenn nodded, eyes on the half-light where sea turns to night. "You know my injury," he said.

"You know how it speaks to me in chop and swell. I can ride a day. I can ride three if I must. Nassau is more than a day in, and maybe more than three back. I can do short. I can do clever. I cannot do long."

Tyler kept his face the way captains keep their faces, even when the inside of them tries to go the other way. "Say it."

"This is where my journey ends," Wrenn said, as if admitting to a small sin. "For now. I'll not be dead weight on a deck that needs speed."

O'Connell came up slow and stopped a step away. He had known it before Wrenn said it. He had the sort of eyes that see where a man will be before he steps there.

"You owe me a drink, James," O'Connell said, to keep his own voice from going wrong.

"I owe you two," Wrenn said. He managed a smile that meant you were a fool and a friend, and I am grateful.

Jenkins arrived with a small, folded paper he was not reading; he folded and unfolded it because his hands wanted a task. "You'll stay with Talbot," he said, not asking.

"For a week," Wrenn said. "Two if the air still smells bad. Then I go home."

Tyler turned his head. "Home is a large word," he said quietly.

Wrenn's mouth went thin.

"Port Royal is full of holes. I know more of them than most. If I stay here, I am a man sitting with his back to a door. If I go back, I can put a hand on things that matter. Sarah's letters won't walk themselves.

The man who carries them won't run forever without help. There are still lines I can pull without making the bells ring."

"And there are hands waiting for your wrists," Tyler said.

"There always were," Wrenn said.

"We came into this with our eyes open. Don't make me proud of you and then treat me like something breakable."

O'Connell grunted. "I'll not call you breakable. I'll call you stubborn and worse words after. But I hear you."

Cobbs joined them, looking like a man who disliked any talk he couldn't punch. He held out his hand in his plain way. Wrenn took it.

Cobbs squeezed once, hard enough to say be alive.

"If Ned finds you first," O'Connell said, using Norton's Christian name like it tasted sour, "buy him a drink with my coin and throw it in his face."

"I'll do something more boring," Wrenn said. "Boring is how men like me live longer than we should."

Tyler put a palm on the rail. For a moment he saw the little room over the cooper's yard, the bottle with wax at its mouth, the copy that had moved across a bench, a woman with a green scarf who had not looked up. Nothing in this life happened alone.

"What's your plan, exact," he said. "Say it out loud. Let it make sense."

Wrenn did not fumble for it. He had been thinking since

morning.

"I sleep under Talbot's roof where his name works as a wall. I keep to rooms with two doors. I speak to one man to fetch the long road runner making sure he's paid twice before he leaves and once when he returns.

I wait until the town looks a different way. Then I take the back boat to Saint-Domingue and from there a small sloop to Port Royal. No straight path. No one proud moment. A lot of dull minutes. My favorite kind."

"That's three crossings," Jenkins said. "Your leg will shout."

"It can shout," Wrenn said. "I won't be on a weather deck long enough to hear it."

Tyler looked out over the water. The frigate lay where it had lain all day, a patient, heavy thing that moved men's lives by being present.

"If you are taken," he said, and the words hurt his mouth, "there will be no escape."

"I knew that since our first meeting in Port Royal, when you said you were in troubles," Wrenn said. "I will not say names, should the worst come to find me."

"You deserve more than this," Tyler said, and hated himself for the line as soon as it came out. Men do not always say the correct brave things at the correct brave times.

"I deserve exactly what I walked toward," Wrenn said, and his voice was kind. "We all do."

They stood like that another minute, and then O'Connell could not stand his own heart any longer. He clapped Wrenn on the shoulder and said, "Go to your friend and let him call you an idiot for me."

"He already does," Wrenn said.

They put him over the side in the skiff after dark. No fuss. No words you wish you hadn't said later. He raised a hand once and let it fall. The water on that side of the island was quiet. It took him in like a man the sea already knew and did not dislike.

Tyler watched the small shape until the night ate it. He kept his jaw still and his eyes on the line where sea turns into nothing. When he spoke, he did not raise his voice.

"We sail," he said.

Pike said, "Aye." The brigantine turned her head away from the bright side of the island and moved for the dark.

They left as a shadow leaves a room when someone opens a door. No trumpet. No wave. The brigantine slid northwest on a wind that did not ask questions.

Hog Island sank behind them to a low, sleeping line. The night ahead was clean. If you have ever felt a deck breathe when it finds the stride it likes, you know how the ship felt.

Tyler stood the first hour and the last hour of the night with O'Connell, because a captain who is not a saint can still be stubborn.

They spoke little. When they did, it was about the wind, not their thoughts.

"Two days we listen and vanish," O'Connell said, like telling the night their promise so it would hold them to it.

"Two days..." Tyler said.

"Jack will hear," O'Connell added, and did not explain how men like Jack hear. Some things you do not speak into the air.

Far back under the darker side of Tortuga, Wrenn took the opposite road. Talbot's man met him at the edge of a warehouse that leaned like it had learned something it did not want to share.

The man's face was one of those faces that do not remember themselves. He led Wrenn through a door that had learned to open without creaking, across a room where things had learned to be other things, and into a small place with a table, two chairs, and a shelf that held more dust than books.

Talbot came late and alone, which is how careful men come when they still like themselves. He looked Wrenn up and down once, not rudely.

"You have the sense to stop moving when your bones complain," Talbot said. "Good. Sit."

Wrenn sat with a sound he couldn't help. Talbot poured water and didn't make a sermon of it.

"You'll hide here," Talbot said. "Three days, five, a week. If you set foot outside in daylight, you do it because you want me to slap you."

"I need a runner," Wrenn said. "The long road."

"You'll have him," Talbot said. "The one who likes to pretend he is slow but isn't. You'll pay him twice and I'll pay him once after that, so he remembers who read the road for him. No chalk. No marks. Just feet."

"I'll go back," Wrenn said. "When the air in town smells like something else."

Talbot leaned his wide back against the door, pale linen clean in a place that was not.

"Back to Port Royal," he said. That was not a question.

"They need a hand on the threads," Wrenn said.

"Sarah can't pull all of them. The boy who carries letters can't carry mine too and still have breath. The man who reads walls with his fingernails can't be everywhere."

Talbot rolled his mouth and looked away. "Captain Davies is

in the roadstead with a frigate that thinks too well of itself," he said.

"It is not polite to make me speak kindly of any English captain, but the boy moves quick. He has a good dog at his heel. Greaves, they call him. I have seen the dog's teeth."

"I have seen worse," Wrenn said, which was a kind way of lying to yourself.

"You are a man who wants to die in his own bed," Talbot said. "Which is rare around here. Pretend harder. Go slow. If you see a boy whistle the wrong hymn, go the other way."

"I taught him that," Wrenn said. "He'll change it now that I've said the words out loud."

Talbot set one big hand on the shelf and said nothing more. He did not like goodbyes. Men like him keep their kindness folded small, so it does not get dirty. He left the room with a nod that held a month's worth of advice.

That night Wrenn slept on a mattress that remembered too many backs and did not complain. He woke before dawn because men do when they have made a plan.

Talbot's man brought him to the back door and pointed him toward the lane that did not want to be a lane.

The plan was a simple one: the Saint-Domingue coasting sloop at first light, a quiet run to a place with a French name that sounded like a cough, then another small deck under his feet toward home. He had done worse twice and lived to tell no one. He stepped out.

The alley smelled of fish, salt, yesterday's smoke, and the iron smell the sea puts on metal before the day is born. He took three steps unremarkably. The fourth step met a shadow that moved.

"James Wrenn," a voice said, and made his name sound like a

lesson and a list.

He turned and saw Greaves first because Greaves had a way of letting his hat do the talking.

Behind him two men too tidy to be locals. Beyond them, in the mouth of the alley, a corporal from the *Compagnies Franches* stared into the middle distance with the bored patience of a man whose pockets had been reminded of something they had forgotten.

"Captain Davies wants a word," Greaves said. His tone carried the polite knife we had heard before.

Wrenn weighed running. His leg answered the wrong way.

He could run five steps and then not the sixth. He could punch once and then not again. He could be clever and loud and be inside a boat he did not own in three minutes, or he could be clever and quiet and still have his teeth in his head when he needed to speak later.

"Then bring me to your Captain," Wrenn said. "I'll give him two words and then I'll need to sit."

Greaves did not smile. "You'll have a bench," he said, and signaled.

The men closed in without touching him and moved him down the alley and into a waiting boat.

Somewhere a coin clicked on a plank, and the French corporal found something very interesting to look at in the sky.

They rowed with the short, neat strokes of men who had been told to be a tide, not a splash.

Wrenn kept his face the way he had kept it all week. He let his left hand lie still over his ribs where he always kept nothing and where once, just now, an oilskin-wrapped book had lain inside a sleeve.

He let his jaw unclench because a clenched jaw tells men the wrong story.

The frigate loomed larger. She had not changed since morning or any morning before that. She had the patient weight of a thing that has turned many men's minds and will turn more.

On the quarterdeck, Davies stood with his hands behind his back, not imitating Tyler—never that—but wearing his rank like a coat that fit.

He watched the boat come up and set his mouth in a line that said he was ready to be calm and unkind.

"Mr. Wrenn," he said when the men brought him aboard. "We have questions."

"Ask them while I am sitting," Wrenn said, and did not look at the faces on the guns or the lines that remembered his hands from another life.

He kept his eyes on the horizon and thought of a boy who could write a line neat three times in a row and of a woman who sewed truth into cloth so that men would not see it until they had to.

They moved him below without a rope. Ropes leave marks. Greaves closed the door with that little neat click he liked.

Wrenn sat on a bench and let his leg do its worst. He counted slowly to fifty and then back down to one. The habit made the room feel bigger.

Out at sea, the brigantine felt a wind shift and took it, shouldering on toward Nassau where names do not stay written long unless they are carved with a knife.

Tyler kept his eyes forward. He did not hear a bell or a door or a man's careful mouth closing like a book. He just felt the world tilt him onto a road he had not chosen and made himself walk it anyway.

Far behind, Tortuga forgot what had happened in one of its alleys. That is what islands do to keep from breaking under the weight of every small thing.

And in Port Royal, a man who liked good rooms and lime and paper woke from a clean sleep and did not know that a piece on his board had moved closer to him without his hand on it.

CHAPTER XII

Knots Tighten

They put Wrenn in a small room below the quarterdeck with a bench, a jug, and a square of light that moved across the planks as the ship swung to her cable.

Greaves took the door with the settled patience of a man who preferred action to talk. Davies came in with a notebook and the look he wore when he'd already decided how the day ought to go.

"Mr. Wrenn," he said, hands behind his back. "You know why you're here."

Wrenn kept his eyes on a knot in the tabletop, like a man weighing a nail. "Because your ship cooks better coffee than the Governor," he said.

Greaves twitched. Davies did not. His voice stayed neat, like lists on a clean page.

"You aided Captain Tyler in avoiding lawful arrest. You moved notes, arranged meetings. You know where he is going and with whom." He let the last word sit.

"Who are the runners. Which doors open."

Wrenn reached for the cup, drank, set it down. "I know the wind changes," he said.

"Names," Davies said. "Places. Tell them now and spare yourself. William Tyler made his choice and dragged you along with him. Be clever now and stop protecting a traitor."

Silence. The ship creaked. Wrenn's mouth tugged once, not quite a smile.

Greaves pushed off the jamb. "We can do this soft or the other way," he said.

Davies cut him a look: not now. He leaned his knuckles on the table.

"You took an oath, Mr. Wrenn. So did I. Duty to the Crown. Duty to the captain. Do it. Tell me what you've built."

Wrenn looked up finally. "My duty is to the truth," he said. "That's why I can't give you what you want."

"You believe Tyler," Davies said. "You believe there's rot in Port Royal." No heat in it. Only a statement, like marking a figure in a margin. "You may be right. You may be wrong. Either way, you will not help me find him."

Wrenn shrugged with his good shoulder. "You're quick."

Davies straightened, closing the notebook without having written a line. Facts first, he thought; the facts were late, and Norton was fast.

The decision was clean in his voice. "We will take you to Port Royal. Mr. Norton has time I do not and methods I do not prefer." To Greaves: "Two men on him at all times. Water and food. No one talks to him."

"Aye, sir."

They moved him to a little cabin with a fixed bunk and a bolt that slid with a sound you could feel in your teeth. The frigate lifted to the long swell and settled.

His leg ached in the way old injuries remember cold. He lay and listened to the ship: the small thunder of feet on the deck above; the voice of the bosun like a rope pulled through a hand; the talk of water on wood, steady as breath.

At dusk Davies came back, alone this time. He did not sit. "You're not a fool," he said.

"So you understand me: I do not enjoy this. I have a job and I will do it. And if you force me to trade your one life for the safety of twenty," referring to the crew Tyler is leading into whatever he planned, "I will trade it. That is duty."

Wrenn looked at the deckhead. "You chose your wall to lean on," he said. "I chose mine."

Davies nodded once as if that was what he had expected all along.

"Very well." He rapped twice and left. The bolt slid again. They weighed at dawn. Canvas climbed. Blocks talked.

The town slid away astern like a story someone else was telling. Wrenn slept in thin strips and woke with the taste of lime and salt in his mouth. Twice Greaves brought him to the air for ten minutes and let him look at a horizon that did not care about men.

On the third morning, Jamaica lifted out of the haze, blue and green and heat. The frigate stood in under easy sail, came to anchor in the roadstead off Port Royal, and let her decks go still.

"Up," Greaves said at the door. They walked Wrenn ashore between two neat files of red coats and up the steps to the Governor's rooms.

Davies wrote a line in a clear hand—*Prisoner Wrenn, for questioning. Urgent*—and did not hand it to Norton. He handed it to Wrenn.

"Give him this," Davies said. There was a look with it Wrenn could not quite read: regret, perhaps, or simply the relief of having passed a hard task into someone else's hands.

They took him through, and the door closed with softness,

that meant money had paid for the hinges. Wrenn felt for the first time in days that he was colder than the air around him.

Davies stood a moment in the corridor and looked at the polished wood that meant influence, at the clerk with the clever hands, at the guards who watched without looking. He had delivered the piece the Governor wanted.

He turned back to the quay where the frigate waited, a tidy patience on her lines. "Make ready," he told Greaves when he reached the gangway. "Stores by noon. We sail again at first light."

Greaves nodded and went to the lists. Davies stood at the rail and let the sun lie on his face. He had thought once that doing right would feel like clean water. It did not. He went below and made his books look like it did.

Norton received Wrenn in a room that looked like an argument between a barrister and a barber: plain table, plain chair, a bowl that smelled of lime, a seal next to it whose brass was so polished you could see what kind of man you were in it if you wanted to.

Norton smiled with his mouth, not his eyes. "Mr. Wrenn," he said, as if welcoming a guest to a clean house.

"We have walked the same streets for years and never said hello. Let's do that now."

Wrenn sat when told. He folded his hands because it gave them something to be that wasn't fists.

Norton's questions began small and tidy. "Where is Tyler headed? Where is his wife hiding? Which entrance to the tunnels behind the ropewalk—if any of those old tales were ever true—still opens without a bar."

Wrenn took the water when it was offered and said nothing.

He closed his eyes when he was allowed to sleep and opened them again with the same quiet face.

On the second day Norton stopped telling polished stories and started using the room like an instrument. He took the chair away and made Wrenn stand until his bad leg sang. He mentioned Sarah once, and only once, as if laying a scalpel on a tray where it would be seen.

Wrenn's jaw clenched, then unwound. Norton watched the muscle jump and made a small, neat tick on a page that had no heading.

"Very well," Norton said at last, in the tone of a man satisfied with a column of figures.

"You are not large, Mr. Wrenn, but you are heavy." He set the seal down as if it were a period at the end of a sentence. "I will not waste more time with you."

The order was short and unornamented. It moved through Port Royal faster than weather. A scaffold went up in the square in an hour because men had built it before and kept the pegs in a bucket.

The town filled because squares always do. Those who had to pass through slowed without deciding to. Those who liked endings came early. Those who feared beginnings came anyway because fear has a way of guiding feet.

They read the neat words that make a death look like a clerk's job: Aiding a deserter; obstructing justice; refusing lawful instruction.

Order issued under the Governor's emergency decree—curfew and obstruction—countersigned by the Provost Marshal. No flourish. No sermon.

Norton stood where he could see without being seen, the way

men who like control prefer their days.

Wrenn climbed the steps with his back straight and his shoulder stiff. If he had a prayer, it was the kind that does not need air. He looked at no one.

Someone in the crowd coughed. Somebody else counted under his breath because numbers make nerves behave.

The rope went where it always goes. The trap answered with the dull sound that turns breath into memory. A bird on the church roof lifted and settled.

Two women who had not meant to watch found they had; and hated themselves for it.

A runner we had seen before arrived too late to be spared and too early to be excused. He left at once with his hat in his hands and his feet loud on the stones. He had an upstairs door to tap at with two fingers and a woman to tell in a voice that did not crack because there were children sleeping in the same room.

Ruth took the boy by both elbows and held him upright until his shoulders stopped shaking. Sarah listened and did not cry the way stories pretend women do.

She made a small sound that sat between her and the wall and stayed. When the boy's throat would work again, Ruth put coin in his palm and sent him down the back steps with a stale crust and a warning to use only alleys where laundry hung because people who plan arrests do not like to get linen dirty.

Sarah picked up the letter she had been writing and did not seal it. She slid it under the mattress where heat and breath would fade the ink. "No more," she said. "Not now."

"Not now," Ruth agreed, because agreement was the only gift that did not make a mess. "We keep small. We make bread. We wait for holes to open."

They washed the floor twice because there is little else to do when a town puts a rope in the square. Ruth kneaded. Sarah swept.

The children slept because children will, even with thunder in the next street.

Norton washed his hands with lime in a bowl he liked because it was heavy and clean. He did not think about Wrenn again. He had pirates to pay, ledgers to alter, guards to move, and a captain to catch. He did not look out the window where the scaffold leaned against the sky like a line on a plan.

Davies heard of it by a note left folded on the quarterdeck slate: *The prisoner refused all; sentence carried out.*

He stood looking at the words as if they would change if he breathed differently. He put the note in his coat pocket and did not throw it away then called for sails and made the ship ready because that was the part of the day he knew how to do.

Greaves tightened his jaw and said nothing. Men who had seen too much said less than men who had seen little, and then only to repeat orders.

The square emptied the way it had filled: by forgetting on purpose. A cartwheel left a rut. A woman with a basket stepped around it. The world kept the shape it had chosen.

The Mercy Anne – Nassau....

Nassau was a grin with too many teeth. It stank of fish left too long on cheap wood, tar steeped in sun, sugar rotting sweet under canvas.

The harbour was a forest of masts and bad ideas. Men laughed louder than their jokes because that was how you signaled you were not afraid to be here.

The brigantine, *Mercy Anne*, came in by the Hog Island side and dropped her hook in clean sand where men in coats were too lazy to row.

Pike ran the deck like it was any town and he was allergic to drama. "No flags," he said. "If a man waves, you don't know him."

Crew stayed aboard. Officers ashore in pairs with pockets light and eyes open, back by nightfall to the same place by the same path. The hands were told to keep their feet off the quay for two days. Rules keep blood inside bodies.

Pike gave Tyler three places to start. "Sailmaker by the old well with bottle scars on both cheeks," he said. "He has patched more lies than cloth. Rope seller at the bend who knows everybody's debts. Woman at the stall with bread like masonry and news that's better."

"Ask for odd weather," Pike said. "Don't say *Valiant*. Don't say British. Let them say it if it's real." They split.

Tyler and Pike walked edges; never down the middle of a street, never against a wall where a knife could be love.

They bought thread and three nails and the right to ask a question. They got stories: a fog bank that came and went like a spoiled child; a sail too large for its mast seen north of Eleuthera; a cousin who swore his cousin had seen a ship-of-the-line where no ship-of-the-line could take a breath. Names slid like fish. Facts clanked like bad coins.

O'Connell and Jenkins worked the other side. They took turns at a pump handle and let old men water the talk.

A pilot with the hands of a man who had not sailed in a year told a tale about a patch of water where the light walked wrong at noon.

Jenkins didn't write a thing. He looked into the man's eyes and kept the picture in his head.

Cobbs paired with Mathurin, the Kreyol topman Pike trusted. They leaned on posts and watched who watched them.

Mathurin had the gift of seeing the back of a man's eyes without seeming to look at his face. He noticed two men in yellow neckcloths who were not sailors and did not try to look like anything else.

"They look without looking," he said. Cobbs grunted and did not turn his head.

At the end of the first day, they met by the boat path behind Hog Island; a scrap of beach where mangroves wrote their names in salt. No crew, just officers.

They took stock: three rumors that might be the same rumor; four faces not to trust; a pilot's patch of wrong light North-by-east that felt more like weather than a plan.

"Salt piles tomorrow," Pike said. "Men who load salt see everything. They hate fog because it steals hours. If there's truth, it's in their mouths."

Day two ran the same lines. Tyler and Pike got handed a chart scratched on a sail rag; the marks were drawn by a drunk with confidence.

O'Connell nearly paid for a story until Jenkins touched his sleeve and the man telling it repeated his lie with a different harbour.

Cobbs and Mathurin saw the yellow neckcloths again, farther off, still not looking.

By evening they had nothing you could put weight on. Pike stood with them under a broken wall where crab grass had climbed, light going, harbour choosing which face it would wear for the night.

"We can keep at this until it's part of us," Pike said. "It's dust."

"Tomorrow one more pass and we cut away," Tyler said. He hated wasting time more than he hated most men.

O'Connell's jaw worked. He liked to win his days. He hadn't.

Jenkins looked like a clerk whose columns would not sum and was offended by the numbers themselves.

That was when two men stepped out, pistols covered by coats, mouths unsmiling. Yellow neckcloths. Not boys. Not drunk.

Calm like men who have worked the same trick often enough to prefer boredom.

"Gentlemen," the taller one said, his accent a scrape of Dutch dragged through salt. "Hands where I can see them. We'll all keep our good looks."

Pike's mouth bent. Something in him refused to be told by this place. "No," he said, and moved.

The shot was close. The sound fell against the broken wall and came back smaller.

Pike took it in the chest like a man who had been hit before and did not care for it.

He went over backward without a word, hat rolling to the edge of the path and stopping like it had hit a thought.

O'Connell took half a step toward the shooter and stopped because the second pistol was already pointing to where his step would end.

Cobbs went still in the way rocks do when gravity remembers them. Jenkins raised his hands like a man who wants to live long enough to be useful.

"Next one is for a throat," the tall man said. "Walk."

Tyler's body wanted to do a thing, his head told it not to. He looked once at Pike, and only once, and put what he saw away like a knife wrapped in cloth. He met O'Connell's eyes.

The Quartermaster's anger was a line pulled too tight to sing. Cobbs' face did not change. Jenkins' gaze flicked to the pistols, the feet, the exits, and settled. They walked.

The harbour fell behind as if it had never wanted them. The two men in yellow neckcloths led without shoving, which was somehow worse.

The path narrowed to scrub, opened to rock, narrowed again. The trees held the heat and the smell of last night's rum.

By the time the last bell before full dark rang down by the quay, they had crossed something that did not want to be crossed and stepped into a place that had been hurt and left standing. News paid to travel arrives thinner.

The ruined church sat on a rise with its roof torn open like a wound long healed. Bats had taken the rafters; salt had taken the sharpness off the stone; somebody had dragged pews into a circle and set them like chairs in a poor man's parlor. Lamps burned low, more shadow than light. The jungle pressed close, listening.

Men waited there the way men wait who choose their own hours. A pair with long guns lounged near the broken door. Another smoked and watched the trees watch them. No one swaggered. They did not need to.

A man in a good coat sat on the altar step with one leg straight and one knee up, like a carpenter resting his back. He was thick through the chest, beard trimmed short, hair pulled back.

There was a pale scar at his temple that made your eyes

return to his face even after you told them not to. When he stood, he did not hurry. Some people use speed to look dangerous. He did not need to.

"Welcome," he said. His voice had the roll of the North Sea somewhere, iron under it.

"I am Eric von Smit. If that name means nothing to you now, it will by the time the lamps burn down."

He walked a lazy half-circle around them, close enough to see the leather creased on a belt, far enough not to tempt a hand.

"Your friend chose," he said, tilting his head toward the harbour.

"He's dead for it. Don't make the same mistake."

Tyler held his ground. "What do you want."

Von Smit's mouth moved in something that was not a smile. "To see if you belong to me or to someone else."

"Joe Cunningham?" O'Connell said, because he could not help himself.

"Your mouth will get you killed," von Smit said mildly. "Yes. My captain. You've heard of him… Good. Here's another name: Norton." He said it like a man tasting something rich and finding it rancid.

"The Governor's pet knife. He pays some men to look away. Sometimes he forgets to pay. We forget to be loyal."

He sat again on the step as if they had bored him already.

"You are men he wants," von Smit said.

"He did not send us. He would pay if I gave you to him. He would also pay if I gave him a thing he wants to hear." He lifted the shoulder.

"I do not like getting paid one way. It makes a man lazy."

"Is this a bargain or a sale," Tyler said.

"Accounting," von Smit answered.

"I keep you where I can see you. You work for me while I decide what you are worth to another man. That way I earn twice: from your labor and from his interest."

He nodded to the two with pistols. They eased back a step like men who had been told the ledger now had a different line to carry.

"Work," O'Connell said, tasting the word. It sounded like a dare.

"The worst of it," von Smit said, pleased to be plain.

"Bilges. Weed scrape. Slush and salt. Rope tar to the elbows. You'll breathe vinegar before you breathe rum.

The bosun will use you until you creak. You will not leave the deck without him saying so. You will not argue with what he says. That keeps you honest and keeps me entertained."

Jenkins' voice stayed even. "And while we turn into deck-apes?"

"While you work," von Smit said, "a man of mine will carry a line to Mr. Norton at Port Royal—his office, not his front door. The line will say I have something that interests him: a man with a Navy head and a face his patrols have been walking in circles for.

He may buy the man. He may buy the news. He may buy both. I am polite. I give him a choice."

"You sell us," O'Connell said.

"I lease," von Smit corrected, almost cheerful.

"Short term. Two days. Three if the wind goes sulky. If Norton offers less than you are worth, we do different sums.

I cut him out and take payment elsewhere. If he offers more, you will be warm and fed upon his road before you find the words to object."

Tyler looked at him and at the scrub that showed a cut lane down to water, where men had already learned to walk quietly.

He weighed what violence would buy and what it would cost. The pistols were relaxed but not unready. The long guns by the door did not move because they didn't need to. There are sums a room writes for you.

"Terms," Tyler said.

"If we are your labor for a day, we are not your trophies for a year. No brand. No marks that make other men ask whose cattle we were."

"I am not a romantic," von Smit said.

"I am a trader. I do not waste stock. You will be men when you leave me. Dirty men, but men."

Tyler saw O'Connell's jaw ask to be a fist. Cobbs' stillness said ugly but work.

Jenkins lifted his chin the fraction that means a man will not like a thing and will do it anyway because it is the right bad choice. Tyler gave von Smit nothing with his face. "Agreed," he said.

Von Smit stood. He stepped into Tyler's space until the leather of his boots creaked. He smelled faintly of soap and gun oil, and a spice Tyler could not place.

"Then you will report to my bosun at bell two," he said. "Name of Van Linde. He thinks God gave him the sea and forgot to charge him for it.

He will meet you at the lantern rail of the brig *Grietje*. She lies under the lee of the customs wall with her yards squared like a vain woman. He will give you a bucket and a brush before he gives you air."

"And if we forget to report?" O'Connell asked.

"Then a different man meets you," von Smit said, "with fewer words. And I send Norton a different line: that a gang of fools with a Navy polish ran from me before they learned how to earn their keep. He will still buy that, but for less, and I dislike taking less when there is more to take."

Tyler did not look away. "And if Mr. Cunningham's boys come sniffing while we are under your hand?"

"Golden Gang is not my concern unless they become it," von Smit said.

"If a yellow scarf looks at you wrong tonight, he isn't mine. If he touches you, break the hand you used and the other for balance. Quietly.

Don't break the man. He might owe somebody I also trade with."

He waved a hand. The pistols turned into shadows because their owners had learned how.

"You'll go back the way you came," von Smit said.

"Use different footprints. Tell the truth to no one. At bell two, you belong to Van Linde's temper. At dusk tomorrow, you belong to my patience. If Norton answers faster than I think, you will belong to a carriage with curtains. If he answers slower, you will belong to buckets and brushes. I do not care which; both pay."

Something in Tyler loosened because a choice, even an ugly one, is still a thing a man can hold. He nodded once.

"We work," he said.

"You do," von Smit agreed. He said it like a blessing withheld.

They took them out through scrub that did not want to be walked, the jungle pressing in like a man at a crowded bar.

The harbour lights looked close and far, as they always do on nights when someone else owns the dark.

Somewhere behind, a runner peeled away on a goat track with a folded paper under his shirt and a name he was forbidden to say out loud.

He would find a sloop with a clean wake, and the sloop would find Port Royal, and Mr. Norton's clerk would find a reason to cough before knocking on his master's door.

Halfway down the path O'Connell finally let air out. "You mean to let a man like that put a bosun over us," he said.

"I mean to live past tomorrow," Tyler answered. "And I mean to know whether Norton wants the man or the news. Both tell us how he is thinking."

"Van Linde," Jenkins said, turning the name as if it were a coin he had to accept. "He the kind that counts the strokes of a brush?"

"He will count to a number that proves something to him and to nobody else," Tyler said.

"We will give him that number and not one more."

"And if Norton's runner is fast," Cobbs asked.

"Then we change ships before we change shirts," Tyler said.

"No speeches. No stands across the deck. Down the ladder. Out." He did not say where. Men become superstitious when they must. He carried the plan in his head like a bird he did not wish to frighten.

They came to the edge of Nassau's noise. A bell marked the hour like a man clearing his throat. The path to the skiff looked like nothing special. The night did not care who they were.

They went down it like men who had learned something they had not asked to learn and would use it anyway, because days don't bend for grief and morning makes you choose.

CHAPTER XIII

Two Ledgers

The clock in Norton's outer office had a habit of clearing its throat before it struck. It did it now: one dry click, as if asking permission to speak, then tolled the hour over King Street.

Rain slanted across the panes in blunt lines. Port Royal wore the wet like a uniform.

A runner stood with his hat crushed in both hands, the way men hold a thing when they want a door to stay open. His hair was soaked flat, his chest still jumping from the last sprint.

"From Nassau," he managed. "For Mr. Norton. From a… from a gentleman who prefers trade to weather."

Norton did not reach for the fold. He watched the boy watch the paper, then flicked his eyes to the clerk by the mantel.

"Dry him," Norton said. "Then bring it." The clerk moved.

The boy went to where he was pointed. The letter sat on the edge of the desk, its wax dull with rain, a small, drowned seal that had done its duty.

Norton let the clock claim two more heartbeats before breaking it. The message was a ledger entry wearing a coat:

To Mr. Norton's knowledge: A man of Navy training, wanted by certain officers, presently under my hand. Inquiries welcome. A coffer of silver will speed politeness.

V. S.

Norton smiled with his eyes and nowhere else. The smile did not move the rest of him. He read it again, then a third time, as if words could learn to misbehave if you didn't keep them under glass.

Sevington's portrait stared back from the wall over the map-table—the powdered face of a man who believed in things that used to be true.

"Bring Master Hartwell," Norton said, still looking at the words. "And send to the harbour for Keane."

Hartwell came first—thin, ink-stained, already balancing a sand-shaker as if there would be writing to do. Keane followed with the weather on his coat.

"I need two letters," Norton said.

Hartwell dipped his head. "To…?"

"'V. S.,'" Norton said, tapping the fold with two fingers.

"He calls himself a trader. Treat him as one. Offer him a coffer of silver to be delivered aboard a frigate—*Enforcer* by name—under a flag of safe-conduct within Nassau Roads.

He will like the sound of those words because men like him pretend to adore the armature of law. Tell him the frigate will meet them just before Nassau on Athol Island."

"And the second?" Hartwell asked.

"To Commander Davies," Norton said.

"By dispatch cutter. He will retrieve Tyler alive from Athol Island. He will carry a coffer that holds nothing but air and the shape of men's greed. Tell him to wait for at least three days.

He will be ready to kill this trader and any creature who obeys him if the shape ceases to be convincing."

Keane cleared his throat. "Under a flag of truce, sir?"

"Under a flag of truce," Norton agreed mildly. "If my flag is to be insulted, I prefer to write the insult myself."

Hartwell began to write with the neat economy of a clerk who knows he is being seen. Wax warmed. Sand hissed.

Norton's seal came down—a ship, a crown, a motto that meant whatever the speaker needed it to mean at dinner.

"Your clearance book will sing today," Norton told Keane.

"Backdate what must be backdated. *Enforcer* will have been anywhere I say she has, when I say it."

Keane's mouth twitched. "Then she will have been diligent, sir."

"Diligent," Norton said, "and punctual." He gestured the runner closer and pressed Hartwell's Nassau letter into his hand.

"Find the sloop that forgets to ring her bell. Give this to the man who answers to 'H' and does not write it down. Tell him the carriage has curtains. He will understand."

The boy nodded as if he did. Boys so often do.

Three days east, a cutter found the *Enforcer* in the grey between squalls. She came in hard under a truce flag and a reefed fore, throwing spray across her bow as if she had grown tired of asking the sea for permission.

A signalman pointed. Davies had already seen her.

The dispatch chest came aboard in a canvas sleeve like a priest being smuggled into a bad house.

The marine sergeant signed his name to a receipt he did not need to read, because the shape of order was comfort enough for him.

Davies broke wax with the same care he used to set a pistol back on half-cock. He read in silence. Then he read aloud the parts that were meant to live outside him.

"Coffer," he said to the carpenter.

"Baulked oak, iron hoops, a false tray that opens like a clamshell with one pry. Weight it to twenty-four stone with brick and lead. Fill the hollows with nothing at all."

"Aye," the carpenter said. "Dress it where?"

"In the great cabin," Davies said. "Let men see a thing and they will tell themselves it is true."

He turned to the Marine Captain. "Forty picked, no drums, no pennants. Round shots in the cannons. Fire only after you can explain to your wife why you did."

The Marine Captain allowed himself a breath of a smile. "We'll be eloquent, sir."

"Boats," Davies said to his first. "Two launches, a cutter. Flags ready for truce and anger both. Powder dry."

"Aye."

"The man," Davies finished. "Tyler. Alive. If he is dead, his shadow will weigh more than any of you expect. Bring the man. Leave the shadow."

There were no cheers. The *Enforcer* moved. The wind had learned to stop making speeches around Davies. It did its work.

Nassau made men into proofs. By bell two, Tyler had a bucket in his hand and vinegar in his lungs.

Van Linde watched him the way a fencing master watches an opponent who refuses to lunge first—coldly, with a private admiration that never touched his mouth.

"Brush," Van Linde said, handing him one that was more bristle than handle. "Strokes count."

The bilge had its own weather. They scrubbed until the wood remembered it was ship and not swamp.

Jenkins bled at the knuckles and didn't mention it. Cobbs learned to coil old rope into obedient circles.

O'Connell listened to the ship with his head cocked like a dog that knows the difference between man-steps and trouble. Van Linde counted.

"You'll do," he said at last, as if he were judging a plank. "Not well. Well, enough."

"Happier men," O'Connell muttered, "have heard worse."

"Happier men," Van Linde said without turning, "are ashore."

The *Enforcer* found her waiting place in the lee of Athol Island, a sliver of sand and scrub that seemed to exhale a damp, green breath into the humid air.

She dropped her hooks with a sound like chains being dragged through the teeth of a giant, and then there was only the waiting.

For Commander Davies, the island became a cage of hours. The three days stretched before him, not as time, but as a physical space he was compelled to inhabit, a suffocating corridor between duty and desire.

His orders from Norton were a masterwork of plausible deniability, an elegant trap baited with a box of nothing.

His own desire was a simpler, sharper thing: to see William Tyler in irons, to feel the satisfaction of the arrest, to close the ledger on the man who had become a deserter damaging the Navy's honour.

He stood at the taffrail, the glass ever-present in his hand, though he saw little of the sea. He saw the court-martial. He saw Tyler's face, not defiant, but amused, as if the whole proceedings were a tiresome play.

The duty was to Norton's plan, to the subtle, brutal theatre of the empty coffer and the flag of truce. The desire was to storm the island the moment a sail was sighted, to take Tyler by force and skip the play entirely.

"Patience, sir," his first lieutenant, Greaves, said quietly, joining him at the rail. "The stage must be set."

"I dislike theatre, Mr. Greaves," Davies replied, his voice low and flat. "I prefer gunnery. A direct solution to a defined problem."

"This problem is... ill-defined, sir. By design. Mr. Norton deals in shades of grey."

"I am a weapon in his hand," Davies said, not with resentment, but with cold fact. "But a weapon thinks only of impact. It does not enjoy the aiming." He lowered the glass.

"Three days. An eternity for a man who knows his quarry is just over the horizon."

In Nassau, the runner found the sloop that forgot to ring her bell. The man who answered to 'H' took the letter with fingers stained with tar and did not write it down.

The message travelled through the port's dark veins and found its way to a tall, grim Dutchman in a tavern that smelled of spilled rum and old wood.

Von Smith read Norton's letter once, his face a mask of stone. He appreciated the language: "frigate," "safe-conduct," "Athol Island."

The armature of law. The trader, V. S., in him appreciated the transaction.

The pirate in him noted the specific location, a place of no refuge, a perfect ambush point. But the coffer of silver was a powerful argument against caution.

He sent a boy to find his navigator. "Deliver this to Van Linde, depart now."

Aboard Van Linde's ship, the name 'Athol Island' was a spark in dry tinder.

Van Linde's muttered order to his navigator had been caught by O'Connell, whose ears were sharper than a ship's cat.

The word was passed in the dark, during the scant hours of sleep allotted to them in the sweltering forward hold.

Tyler listened, his eyes open to the blackness, mapping the ship he had come to know as intimately as his own.

He knew the sentry's rotations, the creak of every deck plank, the rhythm of the ship's bell. He knew the men.

He had seen the sullen glances, the simmering resentment in a few of the crew toward Van Linde's harsh discipline.

"Pike is gone. Our ship is taken. Our crew scattered to the winds of this pestilent island," Tyler whispered, his voice a breath against the groan of the hull.

"We are being sailed into the jaws of the Navy. Norton will be waiting. This is not a delivery; it is an exchange. Our lives for a box of silver."

"We're in a floating prison, sir," Jenkins whispered back, his voice tight.

"Guarded, unarmed, and sailing away from the only place we might find friends."

"A prison has weaknesses," Tyler said.

"And guards have dissatisfactions. I have seen two. The Dutchman, De Witt, who Van Linde flogged for insubordination last week. And the Frenchman, , who cheats at dice and is despised for it. They are unhappy here. Their discontent is a tool."

Over the next day, a frantic, hidden calculus took place.

While scrubbing the decks, Cobbs, whose hands were clever and quick, managed to palm a marlinspike, a short, stout spike of iron used for ropework.

O'Connell, during a trip to the galley for the crew's slop, slipped a rusty but serviceable knife from a careless cook. They were not swords, but they were points of leverage.

Tyler approached De Witt as they were coiling lines. The big Dutchman looked at him with suspicion.

"Van Linde trades us tomorrow," Tyler said quietly, his words simple, slow. "To the Navy. For silver. Do you think he shares that silver with you? After the lash he gave you?"

De Witt's eyes narrowed. He said nothing, but the hatred in them was a language of its own.

Later, O'Connell found Guillerme, sharpening a personal dirk behind the water barrel. "A rich man's game, *non*?" O'Connell murmured. "The captain sells his cargo, becomes richer. We get... what? The pleasure of watching his new silver shine?"

Guillerme spat. "He is a pig."

"A change of management could be profitable," O'Connell suggested. "

A ship, suddenly without a captain, needs a new crew. A crew that could vote itself a share of any silver on board."

The offer hung in the air. It was not a plan, but a possibility. A seed of mutiny planted in fertile soil.

The plan was madness, born of desperation. They would go that night. Athol Island was too close.

De Witt and Guillerme would cause a distraction near the foremast, a staged fight. In the commotion, Tyler and his men would overpower the two guards usually posted near their berth.

They would use the stolen tools and the guards' own weapons. Then, to the gunports.

They had secretly plaited a rope from stolen strands, strong enough to bear a man's weight. They would go out through a port on the leeward side, into the dark water.

Their goal was the ship's jolly boat, towed astern. It was a frail hope, a speck of wood on a vast ocean, but it was a chance. And it pointed back towards Nassau.

The night came, thick and hot. The fight erupted on schedule—a loud, convincing clash of curses in Dutch and French. As the watch's attention snapped forward, Tyler moved.

It was not clean. It was brutal, fast, and silent. A choked cry, the thud of a marlinspike against a skull, the desperate scuffle in the dark.

Two pirates lay unconscious. Tyler, O'Connell, Jenkins, and Cobbs were armed now with cutlasses. They moved like ghosts to the gunport.

The rope held. One by one, they slid down into the shock of the warm Caribbean. The water was ink.

They swam, hearts hammering, towards the faint white smudge of the jolly boat. Cobbs used his knife to saw at the towline until it parted with a snap.

They clambered into the tiny boat, shivering, gasping, free. They seized the oars and pulled away into the darkness, the outline of the brig, a monstrous shadow against the star-strewn sky.

They rowed not for the island, but into the shipping lanes, hoping for a friendly current, a merchantman, anything that would take them back to the tangled safety of Nassau.

Van Linde's roar of fury at dawn could have split the mainsail.

The escape was discovered. The missing jolly boat confirmed it.

He turned his rage on De Witt and Guillerme, but without proof, he could only beat them, not hang them. His silver was slipping away.

His only choice was to sail on to the rendezvous. Perhaps he could still bluff. Perhaps the Navy man would pay for the information, for the trouble.

When the *Enforcer*'s lookout sighted the *Grietje*, Davies was on deck in an instant, a hunger in his eyes he could not conceal. The launches were readied; the marines stood to.

Davies himself went across, his uniform crisp, his face a thundercloud.

He faced Van Linde on the *Grietje*'s quarterdeck.

"You have something for me, trader," Davies stated, his voice cutting through the salt air.

Van Linde spread his hands, a gesture of false apology. "There has been... a complication. The merchandise. It became unstable. It is no longer on board."

Davies went very still. The air around him tightened. "Explain."

Van Linde spun a tale of cunning prisoners, of a night-time escape, of their ingratitude.

He spoke of his expenses, his efforts, his trouble. "But I am here," he finished.

"The information of his capture, the pursuit... it must be worth something. A partial payment. For my diligence."

He was still playing the trader, haggling over a broken pot.

Davies listened, and the cold duty of Norton's plan evaporated, burned away by the white-hot fury of his personal desire thwarted.

Tyler had been here. On this ship. In this man's hands. And this greedy, incompetent fool had let him slip away. He had been so close.

"Diligence?" Davies's voice was a whisper, yet it carried to every man on the deck. "You speak to me of payment?"

Van Linde misread the silence. "A smaller sum, then. For my trouble."

Davies's hand moved in a blur. The pistol was out of his belt, cocked, and levelled.

It was not an act of strategy or orders. It was pure, unfiltered frustration, a rage so complete it bypassed thought entirely.

"Your trouble is over," Davies said. The shot was enormous, a single, flat crack that slammed against the sky and was swallowed by the sea.

Van Linde was thrown back against the rail, a look of profound surprise on his face, a dark flower blooming on the front of his shirt. He slid to the deck, his ledger balanced forever. Silence. Absolute, profound silence.

Davies stood, smoke curling from the pistol barrel, his chest heaving. The act was done.

The theatre had ended in a sudden, brutal reality. He looked at the stunned pirate crew. "Anyone else wish to invoice the Crown?" he asked, his voice returning to a deadly calm.

He turned and went back to the launch, the marines following, their boots echoing on the deck. Back aboard the *Enforcer*, the reality of what he had done began to settle.

"Signal the *Grietje* to heave to. She is now a prize," Davies said, his voice hollow.

"We make for Nassau. We will scour that nest until we find him."

It was Greaves who stepped forward, his face pale but resolute.

"Sir. We cannot."

Davies turned a wild eye on him. "What did you say?"

"Nassau is... not a simple port, sir. It is a political matter. We have just killed a man under a flag of truce. We must return to Port Royal. Immediately.

We must report to Mr. Norton. He must be told that Tyler is loose once more, and he must be told... of this." Greaves gestured vaguely astern, towards the body on the pirate brig.

"He must shape the story before it shapes us."

Davies stared at him, the heat of his fury finally cooling into a hard, cold dread.

He had not just failed. He had transgressed. He had broken the unspoken rules of Norton's world. The weapon had acted on its own, and now it had to be returned to its master.

He looked north, towards Nassau, where Tyler was doubtless finding his feet again. Then he looked south, towards Port Royal, and the calculating, silent man who held his fate.

"Mr. Greaves," he said, his voice stripped of all emotion.

"Sir?"

"Set a course for Port Royal."

The helm answered, and the *Enforcer* gathered herself with the weary grace of a fighter called from bed.

Sails shook, filled, and settled. The deck's small sounds returned: boots, blocks, the muted clack of shot in its garlands, as if the ship preferred the language of routine to the taste of what had just happened.

Davies stood at the transom long enough for the last curl of smoke in his mind to thin. He tried to compose the letter he would have to place in Norton's hand.

Words came like stones: "engaged under truce," "provocation," "self-preservation of the Crown's interests." He set each one down and found it colder than the last.

"Sir," Greaves said, softer now.

"I will have Mr. Lyle draft a first if you wish. You can choose your ground with ink before you step on it."

Davies nodded once. "Put nothing false," he said. "But do not let the truth choose its own shirt." Greaves inclined his head. He understood.

Aft of the main, the Marine Captain took his men by the rail and spoke without sermon.

"You saw what you saw," he told them. "You will say what was ordered." It was not a threat. It was a request in the shape of a rule, made by a man who wanted to keep boys from drowning in other people's words.

On the *Grietje*, command did not so much pass as refuse to be left on the deck.

De Witt stepped forward because no one else would, and because Van Linde had taught him with a lash that silence could be a kind of cowardice.

He ordered the body taken below and the decks sluiced. He ordered hands to remain aboard, no sudden movements when the *Enforcer*'s boat returned to place a prize crew.

He did not look toward the spot on the plank where the dark stain insisted on being seen.

The runner, meanwhile—Norton's wet messenger—had run the letter out and found the sloop that forgot its bell because the bell was a debt and debts were dangerous.

The man called 'H' had said "Curtains, is it?" and smiled with only half his mouth. The boy had eaten a heel of bread in a doorway, watching the rain make small crowns in a puddle, and wondered if men like Norton ever small-talked with their own laws when no one was listening.

Southward, the *Enforcer* drove on the long road home, carrying a coffer full of nothing and a cabin full of words heavy enough to break a lesser table. Greaves, in the great cabin, read his draft aloud as if it were a deck order.

"Engaged the vessel *Grietje* under flag per instruction; found trader noncompliant; prisoner not aboard; hostile movement observed; one shot discharged; prize secured. Recommend immediate consultation with civil authority to ensure forms." He looked up.

"Plain, sir. It will carry."

"Forms," Davies repeated. The word felt like a mouthful of dry bread.

"Yes. Mr. Greaves, you have saved me from writing what I feel."

Greaves folded the paper once, crisp. "That is what ink is for, sir. To keep men from drowning in themselves."

The wind held. The ship made her numbers. Men ate, swore, slept, woke. No one mentioned Nassau. No one mentioned the crack of a single shot.

In the great cabin, the coffer sat where Davies had ordered it: iron hoops, baulked oak, an honest lie heavy enough to convince a man's back he had earned his pay. He did not sit. He would not sit until he had handed Norton his sin wrapped in grammar.

Night found Tyler and his three in a seam of water darker than the rest. The jolly boat was a stubborn cork; every small wave insisted on meeting them personally.

O'Connell counted strokes under his breath until counting stopped being useful and became a punishment. Jenkins's hands, already raw, now wore new skins of salt. Cobbs worked the little boat as he would a stubborn piece of iron: without complaint, with small, certain changes in pressure.

They ate nothing. They drank what the night gave them: a palm's worth of rain caught in the turned-up hat, a shared swallow from the bailer when it happened to forget its usual job.

A fish jumped. Jenkins flinched and then laughed once, short. The sound was wrong on the water. They let it go.

By grey light, a smear of sail showed like a thumb across the horizon. Not Navy—no order in the cut of it—some small Nassau boat working the morning.

Tyler shipped the oars and let the jolly boat lie still so she would look like wreckage and not ambition. The sail drew closer, then veered away with a decision that felt personal.

"Next one," Tyler said, as if there were a schedule and they were merely early.

The tide took them as a parent takes a child who has fallen asleep on a bench; without ceremony, because what else is there to do.

By mid-morning, the colour of the sea had changed the way a face changes when it begins to think of shore. Smell came next: tar, fruit, the clean rot of mangrove.

O'Connell lifted his chin and listened. Somewhere a cock crowed as if the day needed reminding.

"Not the Roads," Tyler said. "Too many eyes. We slide along the back of the island and borrow a shadow." He did not say which shadow. Shadows that could be borrowed often sent a bill.

At dusk, the jolly boat threaded a trickle of green water between roots that reached into the tide like black hands.

A boy in a blue top watched from a bank and then vanished, not because he was alarmed, but because he had been paid, earlier, to vanish at the right time.

The mangroves made a chapel of whispering. O'Connell shipped the oars with a patience he had not earned but used anyway.

"We have until someone decides we do not," Tyler said. "Then we change the decision."

Cobbs found the painter of a fisherman's skiff and tied them in beside it like a second thought.

Jenkins, exhausted past sense, still smiled because the land had agreed to exist. They lay low under cut leaves and the weather's breath and listened to Nassau breathe beyond the trees. It was not safety. It was permission postponed.

Port Royal took the *Enforcer*'s silhouette on the horizon in its usual way, which was to say with gossip. Keane heard first, because harbour gossip is a bureaucrat's barometer: frigate inbound under shortened ensign; a prize in reluctant company.

By the time the ship stood in, he had a quill sharpened to a needle and a ledger open to the page where ships became ghosts and ghosts became histories with dates.

He rubbed two fingers together to feel for the grit of sand he had shaken on wax that morning. It steadied him to know that paper still obeyed when men did not.

Boats went and came. Ropes found bollards. Metal spoke to stone. Davies remained composed by the gangway until the formalities had the decency to be over.

Then he crossed King Street like a man keeping time with a

drum only he could hear.

Back at King Street, Norton kept his hour the way a clock does: faithfully, even if it has learned to cough beforehand.

He had Hartwell lay out a clean sheet and then another, because words sometimes behaved better when they were allowed to think they were not alone.

He did not yet write his name to anything. Not because he feared the ink, but because ownership, taken too soon, makes a poor servant later.

"Master Hartwell," Norton said, "you will have headings ready, nothing more. When Commander Davies arrives, the facts will choose their proper coats. Until then, no coats." Hartwell inclined his head, and the quill waited.

Davies was shown in. He did not sit. He delivered events as a ledger: Athol; the parley; the trader's insolence; the absence of the man they wanted; a single shot; a prize. He handed over Greaves's draft like a blade presented edge-first

Norton read in silence long enough that the clock cleared its throat again. "You have spared me adjectives, Captain," he said at last.

"I have spared the Crown trouble, sir," Davies replied, eyes level. It was neither apology nor boast.

Norton's mouth moved almost into a smile and then remembered itself.

He placed Greaves's paper on the clean sheet Hartwell had laid ready and, only then, dictated:

"Compose for me an account in which the flag of truce is not insulted but tested. In which a trader forgets what courtesy means and remembers it only when someone reminds him emphatically.

In which a commander acts with—" he paused, as if trying on a coat "—brusque prudence."

Hartwell's quill hesitated, then found its pace. Words that would later be called facts began their slow, orderly march toward the future.

"Keane will have the books sing the proper dates," Norton added, almost to himself. "The harbour must remember what we tell it to remember."

Davies inclined his head. He had come to deliver a sin wrapped in grammar; he found it being unwrapped and folded away with the care of a formal shirt.

Outside, the harbour resumed its work. Ships, even the proud ones, prefer not to carry echoes for long; they weigh badly. Inside, the air settled.

"Mr. Greaves," Davies said later, when the formal talk had ended and the corridor cooled the back of his neck.

"Sir?"

"When the gunroom is honest again, send to the tailor."

"The tailor, sir?"

Davies's mouth moved in what, in another man, might have been called a smile.

"If I am to be measured, Mr. Greaves, I will at least be wearing a coat that fits." He looked back toward the door he had just left —toward the room where sentences weighed more than shot.

"And I will stand very straight."

CHAPTER XIV

New Alliances

The mangroves held them until the tide grew honest again. When the light sharpened and the stink of Nassau began to separate into coffee, tar, fruit, and sweat, Tyler let the jolly boat ride the last soft draw out of the green.

They lay still, listening for the one noise that did not belong: boots where there should be sandals, the clink of a pistol butt where there should be a knife handle, the heavy step of a man not worried about who hears him. They heard gulls and men who did not hurry; they heard work.

"Now or not now?" O'Connell asked, extremely low.

"Now," Tyler said, because leaving decisions too long made them turn sour.

They cut the last loop of mangrove root from the bow and pushed out into the filmy light. Jenkins took the forward oar. Cobbs took the after and set a slow, soundless rhythm.

O'Connell kept one palm under the thwart where the stolen knife rested. Tyler watched the tangle of water lanes between hulls, counting sentries by their mistakes; the man who shifted his weight too often, the man who never shifted, the one who laughed for someone else's benefit.

A Golden Gang lookout sat with a clay pipe and pretended the pipe needed more attention than the harbour; he had learned the right pose and not the right habit.

Pike's brigantine lay where she had been forced to lie: off the lower mole, a little apart from the traffic, as if she were a family argument kept on a side chair.

Her yards were braced plain and tidy because men who hire themselves out to a vessel they do not love will still do a thing neatly if it keeps the day short.

Her anchor cable made a line in the water like the stroke of a pen that stopped halfway through a word.

"Still there," Jenkins breathed, relief and fear braided together.

"Indeed," Tyler agreed. "Which is as much trap as gift." They did not go to her.

They trimmed along the back of the waterfront, under the laundries where water dripped in a steady beat from shirts strung on lines, past the coopers' sheds where wood knocked wood, through a raft of smell where a woman threw bad guts into better water and looked unapologetic about both.

They tied up under a rotting stair behind a warehouse that had once been more than honest and now made a living by remembering how to nod.

O'Connell went to look and returned with two facts: Pike's brig had two men aboard from the look of it, both hired, both of the type that gambled with other people's patience; and Von Smit's longboat passed twice in the first hour and not again.

"He thinks we drowned," O'Connell said. "Or he thinks we will drown. Both thoughts drink well."

"Good," Tyler said. "We'll let him buy the round."

They climbed the stair and found a long, dead loft above the warehouse where sacks had once lived and came to understand they preferred the street.

The shutters were warped, the slats split; you could see the anchorage in ragged strips.

They took turns at the gap and ate nothing and drank what the warehouse gave them: stale air and patience.

Cobbs laid on his back beside a sprung plank and touched the planks around him as if he could talk to wood with his fingers.

"She hasn't been handled hard," he said, meaning Pike's brig out there, the lines neat, the sails furled true.

"If Golden hands took her, they would have messed the tidy. Hired hands keep tidy because someone else will check it."

"They sleep by day?" Jenkins asked.

"They don't think danger has the energy to move in daylight," O'Connell said. He did not smile when he said it. "Men who aren't hunted forget where sunset is."

They watched through a day that never quite became respectable. Sun heat pushed old stink up from the planks. A squall tried the air and found the ground too greedy to share, flicked a lash of rain, left. The Golden Gang's longboat did not come again.

On Pike's brig, a man stood once at the rail and scratched his belly and counted the boats that had no interest in him. The other did not appear. The hired kind.

At dusk, two boys chased each other along the plank and stole a peach from a cart and vanished down a lane. A woman sang a halting line and abandoned it without apology. Somewhere, a man swore at a rope and then apologized to it when it obeyed.

"Night," Tyler said, and the word made the room lighter. They did not go at full dark.

They waited for the soft part, when lanterns had been doused by men who were allowed to be careless, when drink had cut courage down to the size of sleep.

When it came, they took the stair down and moved along the shadowed backs of hulls. Cobbs set the oars like a man placing tools back in their box.

They came abeam of the brig's starboard quarter and let the jolly boat kiss her with the barest suggestion of a sound.

"Jenkins," Tyler murmured. "Toes and fingers." Jenkins's hands knew more than their years; he went up the channel of the after chains like a boy climbing an old tree. He leaned, peered, and looked down with his eyebrows.

Two, his face said. One behind the caboose, one in the shadow of the mainmast. Both sleeping the kind of sleep men learn when they trust coins and not orders. Tyler nodded.

O'Connell went up, then Cobbs, then Tyler last, because he had learned not to be the first man over any edge he could help. They touched the deck and the deck agreed to be quiet.

The hired man behind the caboose snored like a man who has been paid to snore and has decided to be worth his fee. The other had a knife loose in his belt that would betray him to any rope he leaned on. He did not lean on any.

"Easy," Tyler said, not because they needed to hear it but because he needed to say it.

Cobbs took the caboose sleeper by the mouth with a hand the size of a Sunday ham and pressed the air out of his argument while O'Connell plucked the man's pistol from his sash and set it down with the care of a surgeon who would rather not meet his own work later.

Tyler knelt by the man at the main and feathered his own blade against the man's throat without touching. The man opened his eyes because the cold in the air changed.

"Speak soft," Tyler said. "Speak true. We are not here to bleed you." The man looked at the dark, weighed it, and chose economy.

"Aye."

"Stand," Tyler said. "Hands where your mother would see them." The man stood.

He did not look brave; he looked like a man at the library of his bad choices trying to pick a short pamphlet.

"Crew?" Tyler asked.

"Two of us," the man said. "Hired to keep her steady and to be here. Owner did not fancy her moored to a quay. That is all."

"Who paid you?"

"A man with a Dutch mouth and a bad eye for small change," the man said at once.

"But his coin was real. He set us aboard and said to keep her neat. That is what we did."

"And what was his instruction if men came for her who knew her name?"

"Had no instruction for that," the man said, and it was almost true.

"Said not our business to ask. Said we could sleep by turns." Tyler let air out slowly.

The brig had not been eaten through with sickness. She had been held, not chewed. A difference.

"You're awake now," Tyler said. "Wake him." He nodded to the man under Cobbs's hand.

"We will talk like men who prefer to count what they have rather than invent new things to lose."

In the great cabin, everything remembered its place. Pike's

compass hung by its string and did not lie. The log-slate had a crooked mark two days old.

A mug had a line of dried sugar at its rim, cut by the tongue of someone no longer present. The hired men sat where they were told and tried to look both harmless and still useful. They achieved half.

Tyler spoke the short version because men in the wrong room deserve no more than that: they had been taken; they had left; the man with the Dutch mouth had made a mistake and then a corpse; the Navy would go home and write the story in a hand it found flattering; Tyler had a place to be and a time to be there.

"You can go," Tyler finished.

"Or you can stay and earn more than you were promised. If you go, you will go in the jolly and keep your faces turned away from questions.

If you stay, you will do what you are told for a little while, then you will go with weight in your pockets.

If you warn any man with a Dutch mouth that we left, the weight will be your own mistakes, and I cannot spend those."

"You Navy?" the man asked, not as an insult but as a question a man asks himself when he doesn't like the answer he suspects.

"I was," Tyler said.

"Now I am the weather between two ships." The man considered and shrugged in a way that said coins and sleep tasted similar when you were tired.

"I'll stay," he said. His mate, revived and sober enough to understand that men who can climb fences quietly should be listened to, nodded too.

"Then do what you were going to do tonight," Tyler said.

"Only cleaner."

By midnight, the brigantine had a pulse again. Cobbs walked her deck like a father looking over a child brought back from a fever.

O'Connell found the little wrongness: a cleat that had been tied by a right-handed man in a left-handed hurry, a coil flipped against its grain and patted them back into truth.

Jenkins ran messages with the silent pride of someone allowed to carry good words. The anchor came in without fuss.

The sails went up with the soft whump that is the opposite of showing off. They put Nassau on their quarter and let the night work.

The hired pair proved what all hired men prove when asked to do a thing straight with someone confident watching: they were adequate and relieved to discover it.

Tyler put one of them on the sheet of the fore and the other at the helm under O'Connell's hand. The man's touch improved at once with the knowledge that someone noticed it.

"Course?" O'Connell asked in the tone of a man who would prefer to spend a life not saying, "we shall see."

"West-by-south," Tyler said.

"Enough to clear bitterness. Then we set for Tortuga." He did not let the word sound like relief. Relief makes fools.

They did not run themselves to bones. Tyler had learned long ago that arriving with men that can still think buys more life than winning a quarter day.

He kept them steady, watching over his shoulder for any stub of sail that suggested someone else had thought to keep the night interesting. None came. The world had other worries.

It took them two days because the wind had opinions and

because Tyler chose to let it have a few without argument.

They ate hard bread and water and something that had once been salted fish. They talked little and slept when told. They did not light lanthorns unless the dark tried to pretend it was a wall.

Cobb's hands, given something to care for, forgot the shape of a borrowed knife and remembered lanyards and thimbles. Jenkins lost the sting in his knuckles without noticing. O'Connell stood with the kind of stillness that is not calm but the absence of fidget.

On the second dawn, the sky tore itself open for a quarter hour and poured light. Tortuga rode the edge of it like a coin catching sun: red roofs, white walls where anyone could afford lime, the slope of the hill where goats made their own laws, the dark scar of *La Sirène's* street running like a promise to the water.

They let the brigantine fall off and coaxed her toward the anchorage with the politeness you give a proud woman in a narrow door.

They chose their hook carefully: not in the line where the Admiralty likes to count, not where Jack's men liked to make a show of their luck, not in the pocket where French captains pretended to be ashore doing penance.

They put her in where a man's eye would skip over her on its way to the gossip it preferred.

Tyler paid the hired men with coins that carried no message beyond weight and nodded toward the shore.

"If anyone asks you who brought the brig back," he said, "say a man who did not have the time to be thanked."

The man grinned because that line could be sold later with embellishments. "Aye."

On the quay, the old smell of coffee and rum and salt met

them like a friend no one had the energy to distrust. *La Sirène* kept one shutter cocked, like a woman lifting her petticoat to catch a breath of wind.

Inside, the same cracked mirror watched the bar as if it despised vanity but kept a ledger for it anyway.

A woman with hair like two ropes and arms that said she could throw you out or hold you up without complaint wiped a board with the kind of care you save for your own possessions.

"Anisette, leave the bottle" Tyler said, because the body remembers a safe word even when the world doesn't mean it this time.

They stood at the end of the bar where the shadow made faces less committed to being recognized. They did not talk about the sea, did not drink.

Talbot did not arrive. Instead, they met a man Jack sent when he preferred to remain someone you ask for rather than someone you find.

He came as if he owned no part of the floor except the bit his boots claimed.

Jack's Quartermaster was a man who had run out of patience for introducing himself years ago; he let the scar on his cheek and the ring on his forefinger do that work. He had a pleasant way of disliking people.

"You'll come with me," he said, not because he believed they wouldn't if asked, but because he'd learned orders are quicker than invitations in rooms with thin walls.

Tyler nodded as a man nods to a road he has walked before.

The Quartermaster led them to the back where the reek of the kitchen disguised better smells, touched the wall where three boards had a different varnish, and slid a hand down a seam that was not a seam until you asked it to be. The wall sighed and gave. They went through.

It was very tidy; secrets usually are. They climbed a narrow twist where the timber had been planed close for men without bellies.

A door took them sideways into a gallery that ran above the tavern like a balcony in a church built by people who liked sin, and there at a table under a painting of a saint no one would have recognized sober sat the man who owned the place and the man who owned the horizon.

Talbot always wore other men's wealth like it was his and you were a fool to think otherwise.

Jack wore his story: a long coat that could hide kindness or knife, the scar that looked like a child had tried to draw a smile on the wrong part of his face, eyes that held more agreements than a court. The Quartermaster stood behind his chair like a polite threat.

"Captain," Talbot said, without the warmth of friendship and without the cold of the opposite. "You make a habit of leaving a room hot and arriving in it wet."

"Mr. Talbot," Tyler said, standing, because he had not yet earned the right to sit. "Jack."

Jack drummed two fingers once and let them stop. "Sit," he said.

"Drink a better drink than that perfume you like." They sat.

A bottle that did not come from *La Sirène's* shelf appeared with the quiet of things that have been too expensive to mention. The glass that came after it had weight.

Tyler did not drink. O'Connell did and made no face. Jenkins pretended to drink and did not. Cobbs drank and set the glass down like it might tell on him.

"We have news," Talbot said. "Some you will not like."

Tyler did not look at O'Connell because looking makes you read a man before the page has been turned.

"Go on."

"Your friend," Talbot said. "Mr. Wrenn. He is dead." The room found that soft silence it gets when information sits down at the table without chairs being moved.

Talbot let the quiet do its work for a breath and then finished the lesson. "By a rope in Port Royal. Officially by order. In truth by Norton's theatre. Public, efficient, and instructive."

Tyler's throat had the feel of a rope in it all at once, the way a man will swallow a story when it refuses to stay where it belongs. He tried to put breath in and found there was no room.

Wrenn had been his friend in all the ways that aren't written on paper: the one who said nothing when saying nothing was the kindest thing you could do; the one who stood by a bad decision and made it survivable; the one who had a way of making a plan feel like luck. And now the world had turned that small loyalty into a spectacle at the end of a rope.

O'Connell touched the table and then took his hand away as if it were hot. No one looked at Tyler and everyone did.

He felt both seen and not helped. He put his hand to his chest because grief is as physical as a blow; he steadied himself because men were watching.

He saw Wrenn's hands, the little scar at the base of the thumb where a bottle had taught him to respect glass, the nail he kept too short so you couldn't know it had once cracked; saw them make some small careful motion like they were about to fix a thing, and then stopped because imagining hands after the rope is a cruelty he would not do to another man.

He did it to himself because he had run out of rules big enough to stop it.

"How," Tyler managed. The word came like a knot pushed through a small hole.

"Greaves sent the papers north," Talbot said.

"Norton arranged the rest. They raised the gallows on the harbour. The order was read. The officers stood straight. Wrenn was hanged."

Tyler's sight went small, like he was looking down the wrong end of a telescope.

He put both hands flat on the table and spread his fingers as if he could hold the wood together and keep the whole building from sliding.

He stayed in that place until his breath remembered it had work. When he spoke, his voice had been filed down to something that liked edges.

"Thank you," he said to Talbot, because gratitude is sometimes the only currency that does not feel like a lie.

O'Connell cleared his throat. "Bad news for bad news," he said, as if the words were stones, he had to arrange carefully.

"Pike is dead."

Talbot did not blink. "I know," he said.

"That is why you are here and not with him. That is why your brig rides where she rides. Mr. Pike did a brave, stupid thing and died in the middle of doing it. Brave men make good stories. I prefer longer stories."

Jack's mouth huffed something that wasn't a laugh.

"Pike bled for a plan that stopped being a plan halfway through," he said.

"The sea doesn't refund effort, only outcomes."

O'Connell lifted his chin. "He died right," he said, because if you do not say a man died right, those who died before will hear you as fail them.

Talbot nodded once. "He did," he agreed.

"And so a debt opens." Tyler looked at the bottle he had not touched.

"I paid you once," he said. "With a book. My account was clean."

"Until you broke it," Talbot said, not unkindly.

"You lost me a captain. That loss stands on your side of the page, Captain Tyler, no matter how the line was drawn. I do not charge interest on grief. I do call a debt a debt."

Jack tipped his head. "We aren't the Admiralty," he said.

"We don't invent fines. We count, and men accept the numbers because they are true."

He waved two fingers at the Quartermaster, who slid a folded paper from his coat and set it on the table. Jack did not touch it.

"Here is what the sum becomes."

Tyler did not reach. "Say it."

Talbot leaned his elbows on the table the way a man leans on a rail when he is about to explain why the horizon is his.

"We have information—a lot of it, and honest. About a ship you care about: *Valiant.*

You have been trying to find her since you realized that the game you are in is being played on two boards. We can set you on a path that leads not only to news but to the ship herself.

There is a path at sea and a path in paper. We know both. We are prepared to give them to you."

"And the other side of the page," Tyler said.

Talbot's eyes warmed a fraction because a conversation that admits terms is an old friend of his.

"You find the *Valiant*, you take her. After that, you give one year. One year of work in my book and Jack's—no plunder for its own sake, no murder. Targeted work.

Documents, seals, letters, tallies. We will put you on cargo that does not exist until the right paper says it does.

We will put you against Norton's hired thieves who wear the word 'pirate' the way a magistrate wears a robe.

You will unmake his arrangements. You will make ours smooth. Twelve months. After that, you are the weather again."

O'Connell sat back. "A year," he said, tasting the length of it. "What happens if the sea decides not to give us a year?"

"Then your debt dies with you," Jack said, plain.

"The sea writes off men better than any banker. We don't make collections on ghosts."

Jenkins spoke because he was young enough to miss one etiquette and old enough to make a better one.

"We don't do blood," he said. He looked at Tyler and hated himself for saying "we," and then did not hate it, because it was true. "We don't kill to make a cart lighter."

Jack's face did a thing that would have been kindness if it had stayed on. "You think we do?" he asked.

He didn't ask to threaten. He asked because he wanted the answer to know what shape to take.

"We know what Norton does," Tyler said, voice even. "He dresses pirates in uniforms when it suits and dresses officers in rags when it suits.

He makes other people's handwriting do his work. He lets fights look like fights so men can tell themselves stories. I will not be the other side of his coin."

Talbot spread his hands. "That is precisely why you are in this room and not a different one with different men." He glanced at Jack.

"Tell him."

Jack sat forward the way a bluff sits forward when truth decides to put real clothes on. "

Norton came to me twice," he said.

"He wanted a partnership. Not the honest kind where men share useful lies. The kind where one man holds the pen, and the other man supplies signatures.

He wanted us to fence his stolen goods. He wanted us to move cargoes that make Kings feel clever: sugar travelling as spice, guns travelling as lumber, slaves travelling as 'souls under ministry.'

He wanted us to be the part of him that could be blamed when the wind changed."

"You refused," Tyler said, making sure of a step he wanted to put his weight on.

"I did," Jack said.

"Because I prefer roads where I know who will try to rob me. Norton prefers roads where he is the robber in disguise, and the guards wave him through because his seal is tidy.

He sets up pirates where he needs a scarecrow and calls it law when it eats a man.

He takes traders who have learned to be careful and makes them careless with promises.

He means to own the cost of doing business in this water, he means to rent out safety and repossess it when a man misses a payment."

Jack looked down into his glass and saw nothing he liked.

"That ruins my trade. That ruins Talbot's. Men who do business need risk they can price. Norton sells surprise. You cannot price surprise and keep your house."

Talbot nodded. "A truce is only good if both sides are frightened of the same thing. Norton is only frightened of being caught without a sentence ready.

He would rather burn a dock than admit a delay. We prefer docks. Docks grow back money faster than fires."

Tyler let the room sit on him. He could feel Wrenn in the place where decisions had always been easier because someone else had been there to say the thing you could not.

He had left Port Royal with a plan that had been half prayer, half map. He had found men who spoke plainly and a price that was both too high and exactly what the situation would bear.

He had promised himself he would not become the man Norton thought he was. He had promised Sarah—he had promised her in the small quiet way you promise a woman when you know she hates the kind of promises men like you have to make—that he would not come back to her with other people's blood on him as if it were work.

A year. Twelve months of taking pieces of paper and the power that sat on them and turning both to better uses than Norton's.

Twelve months of finding men like the Golden Gang and untying their knots by cutting rope, of pushing against a machinery that had decided to make his friends into performances.

"It is not blind murder," Talbot said, reading the thoughts on Tyler's face as if they were printed.

"If it were, you would not be a good hire. It is selective correction. The kind of work that lets other men pretend the world is honest because someone did the dirty calculations when they weren't looking."

"Dirty calculations still dirties the hands that do it," O'Connell said, not hard, not soft.

"True," Talbot allowed.

"But those hands choose the sums."

Jack gestured and the Quartermaster placed a second paper on the table, this one with three names written on it in a hand that had written better names and found them more expensive.

"These," Jack said, "belong to Norton. They wear his seal on their teeth.

They call themselves free captains because a magistrate is lazy and the sea forgives when a man says sorry with coin and will make your year if you take it: three ships, three routes, three letters that make all their theft legal.

Cut their letters, bring me the book that says their cargo is sugar when it is men. Bring Talbot the list that says which harbourmaster closes which eye without firing a shot.

You may have to push a man down a stair and tell yourself he tripped. I am not romance; I am terms."

Tyler looked at the names and did not touch them. He could hear Wrenn's voice the way you hear the sea through a door—a constant, not a speech. He could see Pike's hand, blunt finger on a chart, tapping a line and making it mean: "We will go there" not "We could."

He could feel Sarah's breath on his wrist the last time he had been close enough to forget the air belongs to everyone.

"How long to find *Valiant*?" he asked, because asking about the prize was safer than saying yes to the cost.

"Three weeks," Talbot said, without hesitation.

"If you listen when told… If you ignore the men who wish to give you advice to make themselves feel useful. If you do not stop to argue with someone who wants to teach you a clever phrase."

Jack snorted softly. "He means me," he said.

Talbot allowed himself the ghost of a smile. "Sometimes."

O'Connell leaned forward. "And if we find her and she is a ruin?" he asked.

"If she is a story without a ship to hang it on?"

"Then you have still taken away one of Norton's reasons to stand up straight," Talbot said.

"That is worth more than you think. But she is not a ruin. She is a tool in someone else's hand. I prefer it in yours."

Cobbs cleared his throat, which men rarely notice until it means they are going to speak.

"And the men," he asked.

"The hired kind who don't have a say in who pays them. If we take the paper and the paper stops their bread, what do we make instead?"

"Work," Jack said simply.

"The sea never lacks work. If you take a thief's permit away, the thief can go honest or find a different lie. That part is not our business.

Our business is removing one particular lie from the table, so other men stop choking on it."

He tapped the sheet with the three names. "Norton makes sure these men never go hungry. He feeds them other men's children. He calls it order. You cut his rhythm and make the hunger go where it belongs."

"Which is to Norton?" O'Connell asked.

"If the world were neat," Jack said.

"It isn't. But Norton learns a lesson the way kings do: in public and with the wrong people applauding. He will move slower while he rehearses."

Tyler let himself breathe through his nose the way he did when the ship had found headwind, and he had to consider the kindness of tacking instead of the drama of argument.

He could say no and make this room an enemy or say yes and make himself a different man than the one who had told himself blood was a last resort and not a tool.

He could say maybe and be a kind of coward that he had promised not to be when he had first learned a chart.

"You will want to think," Talbot said, not pushing.

"Good. Thinking keeps funerals short."

"You will want to promise," Jack said. "Don't. Promise when you cannot bear not to."

Tyler set his glass down. He had not drunk. He wanted to. He wanted to feel something warm go into him and tell him he was still a man with a throat. He did not.

"My rule is no blood for its own sake," he said, saying it to the room and to the boy he had been and to the friend who had died and to the woman he still called by her first name in his head when he needed to steady himself.

"I don't break it to make a debt lighter."

"Then don't," Talbot said. "Break Norton's instead."

The Quartermaster shifted his weight, and the floor did not complain. Below, in *La Sirène's* belly, someone laughed at a joke that had been told too often and still worked.

The Saint on the wall looked away as if he had important business with the ceiling.

O'Connell looked at Tyler with a faith that had learned how to disguise itself as practicality.

Jenkins stared at the ragged edge of the paper with the three names and saw in them not men but arrangements, like knots that could be untied if your fingers were clean and your patience better than your pride.

Cobbs watched the bottle and decided he did not deserve more of it.

Tyler closed his eyes for the length of a breath and opened them on the same room.

"We will need your routes," he said to Talbot.

"And the names of the men who watch your routes, the book that holds the hand that writes the names for the harbour. And your Quartermaster for a day. He knows where the floor gives and where it doesn't."

"All that is yours if you lift your hand," Talbot said. "And if you put it down again in twelve months."

Jack's fingers began their quiet tap and then stopped. "We don't own you," he said.

"We're renting trouble. We like your kind."

Tyler felt the decision come toward him like a wave you can't jump because the shore is too near.

You can brace and take it and be standing after, or you can pretend it will go around you and find yourself rolling with a mouth full of sand. He did not speak into it. He let it hit and stood. He did not, yet, say yes.

"Tonight," Tyler said. "We sleep aboard and send no message. In the morning, if the weather permits, we speak again."

"Here," Talbot said.

"Here," Tyler agreed.

Jack stood too. He held out his hand and did not care if anyone thought it sentimental. Tyler took it.

Jack's grip was the kind that says I will let go when you tell me to and not before. He let go.

Tyler turned toward the door and the Quartermaster held it, a courtesy that had probably killed men who mistook it for kindness. The passage swallowed them back; the kitchen air found them; *La Sirène* resumed being the kind of place where complicated things could be hidden in simple ones.

On the street, Tortuga's night made its bargain with the moon.

Back aboard the brig, the water talked against the hull in a way that had always made Tyler think of someone trying not to wake a child.

Jenkins went forward and lay down and fell asleep with his mouth open because he had run out of performances. Cobbs checked a line that did not need checking and checked it anyway because grief and caution are cousins. O'Connell came to the rail and stood where the light from *La Sirène* was a smear on the water and not a beacon.

"You didn't say yes," he said, not a question.

"I didn't say no," Tyler said.

"Wrenn would have said the thing that lets you say yes without lying," O'Connell said quietly.

"He would," Tyler answered. "Which is what makes this harder."

O'Connell watched the smear of light break. "A year is a long time to be clever," he said.

"It is," Tyler said. He could feel the shape of the year in his hands, heavy as a coffer and just as empty until you decided what to put in it.

He could feel Sarah, not as a reproach, but as a human presence that made rooms with promises in them feel smaller. He could feel Norton far away at a desk, writing a version of the world that would make fools of anyone who refused to write their own.

Tyler looked up at the dark and tried to find the same first star Davies had stared at two nights ago without knowing he shared a sky with a man he would hunt. The star was where stars go when men need them; it stayed.

"What will you decide?" O'Connell asked, too soft to be a challenge, too hard to be comfort.

Tyler answered the only way he could answer without becoming a lie in his own mouth.

"I don't know."

A week later – London's Admiralty

London made a different kind of weather. Fog walked streets and pretended it had always had right-of-way. Bells learned to guess at their distances. St. Paul's dome was a rumour you could bump into and apologize to.

Admiralty House wore the fog like a wig it disliked. Inside, the boardroom had the clean cruelty of oak and maps. A stove clicked to remind the room that heat is a choice.

Three Lords Commissioners sat with their coats unbuttoned as if to confess they were human and then changed their minds. The permanent secretary, ledger-nerved and literal, took minutes with an ink that had not yet forgiven anyone.

"Nassau," said Lord Selby, who chaired because he had mastered the art of sounding inevitable.

"Our man in Jamaica reports that one Tyler—late of His Majesty's service—refused to remain where he had been put."

"Mr. Norton's packet," the secretary added, tapping a sheaf with two fingers, "contains: first, schedules for a Kingston convoy over eight weeks; second, a memorandum on irregular fog North-by-east of Eleuthera; third, observation on a customs ledger 'misplaced' at Nassau's wall during a certain forenoon; fourth, a charge-sheet alleging Captain William Tyler's desertion, with request that he be publicly posted as traitor to the Crown; and fifth, Mr. Norton's endorsement that Lieutenant Paul Davies be confirmed in command of His Majesty's frigate *Enforcer*."

Admiral Worth, whose face had been weathered into discretion, made a small sound that could have been approval. Lord Penrith, who distrusted men who smiled for a living, turned Norton's letter as if it might be double.

"Norton proposes we engage Tyler's... expertise," Penrith said dryly.

"Quiet counsel on convoy routes. Payment in coin and latitude. He writes as if he expects to be agreed with by better men than himself."

"He often is," the secretary murmured, earning a glance that would be recorded as silence.

Selby folded Norton's letter exactly once. "Jamaica needs victories that read as prudence. If the gentleman in Port Royal can purchase that with a purse and a line, I am not minded to stand between him and economy."

"The desertion—and 'traitor,'" Penrith pressed. "Strong meat for a colonial table."

"Tyler deserted," Worth said without embroidery.

"If Norton wishes him proclaimed in the islands, let the proclamation bear London's spelling and Jamaica's seal. As for Davies—he will do what the book permits until the book offends him.

He will take Tyler alive if the flag allows it and the wind consents. He will not write poetry in his log about why he did not."

Selby let the room breathe. "Very good. We shall—" he allowed himself a word he used rarely, "—trust Mr. Norton, for the present.

Authorize a public posting in the Jamaica Gazette and at principal harbours: William Tyler, late captain, proclaimed deserter and traitor to the King's peace, to be taken alive if taken at all.

And issue to Lieutenant Paul Davies a temporary commission in command of *Enforcer*, ad interim, to be confirmed at the next Board. Draft the reply accordingly."

The secretary's pen made a sentence that would look like three different things depending on who read it. He sanded it with professional pity.

"What of the *Valiant*?" Penrith asked.

"We will send someone else to find it, keep Davies on Tyler" Selby said.

The board rose in that choreographed way institutions learn after a hundred winters. Outside, the fog revised London into a set of close-up problems. Inside, the reply to Jamaica cooled under wax and a motto.

Two days later, the fog came back to see what had become of its friends. The doorkeeper at Admiralty House opened to a sailor with shoulders like the solution to a simple machine.

The man did not remove his hat. He carried a packet with more caution than its size required.

"For Their Lordships," he said, "from the Indies by clean hands, and quicker than the weather."

The doorkeeper looked at the seal and decided not to ask questions he would later be scolded for.

The packet went along passages that had learned to forget who walked them. It came to rest under Selby's hand with the inevitability of ink.

Wax broke. The outer fold bore a packet mark from *Cap-Français*, the kind clerks trust because it arrives slower than a lie.

The secretary read the outer fold and did not comment on the neatness of the hand because it would have been unkind to the men in the room. He cleared his throat for the record.

"From... Sarah Tyler," he said.

ABOUT THE AUTHOR

Mattia Biscontini

Mattia Biscontini is an hobbyist writer based in the UK and fluent in English, Italian, and Spanish. He works in legal-tech as developer.

Under the Governor's Seal — Book One: The Shape of Power launches his saga of captains, clerks, and the documents that decide who lives and who hangs.

When he isn't writing, Matty plays guitar in a metal band, reads court records for fun, and argues that a good countersign beats a broadside.

Printed in Dunstable, United Kingdom